SHILOH
SEASON

BOOKS BY PHYLLIS REYNOLDS NAYLOR

o—o—o—o—o—o—o—o

Shiloh Books
Shiloh
Shiloh Season
Saving Shiloh

The Alice Books
Starting with Alice

Alice in Blunderland
Lovingly Alice
The Agony of Alice
Alice in Rapture, Sort of
Reluctantly Alice
All But Alice
Alice in April
Alice In-Between
Alice the Brave

Alice in Lace
Outrageously Alice
Achingly Alice
Alice on the Outside
The Grooming of Alice
Alice Alone
Simply Alice
Patiently Alice
Including Alice

The Bernie Magruder Books
Bernie Magruder and the Case of the Big Stink
Bernie Magruder and the Disappearing Bodies
Bernie Magruder and the Haunted Hotel
Bernie Magruder and the Drive-thru Funeral Parlor
Bernie Magruder and the Bus Station Blowup
Bernie Magruder and the Pirate's Treasure
Bernie Magruder and the Parachute Peril
Bernie Magruder and the Bats in the Belfry

The Cat Pack Mysteries
The Grand Escape
The Healing of Texas Jake
Carlotta's Kittens
Polo's Mother

The Witch Books
Witch's Sister
Witch Water
The Witch Herself
The Witch's Eye
Witch Weed
The Witch Returns

The York Trilogy
Shadows on the Wall
Faces in the Water
Footprints at the Window

Picture Books
King of the Playground
The Boy with the Helium Head
Old Sadie and the Christmas Bear
Keeping a Christmas Secret
Ducks Disappearing
I Can't Take You Anywhere
Sweet Strawberries
Please DO Feed the Bears

Books for Young Readers
Josie's Troubles
How Lazy Can You Get?
All Because I'm Older
Maudie in the Middle
One of the Third Grade Thonkers

Books for Middle Readers
Walking Through the Dark
How I Came to Be a Writer
Eddie, Incorporated
The Solomon System
The Keeper
Beetles, Lightly Toasted
The Fear Place
Being Danny's Dog
Danny's Desert Rats
Walker's Crossing

Books for Older Readers
A String of Chances
Night Cry
The Dark of the Tunnel
The Year of the Gopher
Send No Blessings
Ice
Sang Spell
Jade Green
Blizzard's Wake

• The Shiloh Quartet •

SHILOH
SEASON

by
PHYLLIS
REYNOLDS
NAYLOR

Atheneum Books for Young Readers

NEW YORK LONDON TORONTO SYDNEY NEW DELHI

With special thanks to the staff of Seven Locks Animal
Hospital, Potomac, Maryland, for their information and help,
and to Frank and Trudy Madden, once again, for their love
and care of the real Shiloh.

First Aladdin Paperbacks edition April 1998
First Atheneum Books for Young Readers edition April 2013
Copyright © 1996 by Phyllis Reynolds Naylor

Atheneum Books for Young Readers
An imprint of Simon & Schuster Children's Publishing Division
1230 Avenue of the Americas
New York, NY 10020

Designed by Becky Terhune
The text of this book was set in Goudy.
Printed and bound in the United States of America
44 46 48 50 49 47 45 43
The Library of Congress has cataloged the hardcover edition as follows:
Naylor, Phyllis Reynolds.
Shiloh season / Phyllis Reynolds Naylor. — 1st ed.
p.   cm.
Sequel to: Shiloh.
Summary: When mean and angry Judd, who has never known
kindness, takes to drinking and mistreats his dogs, Marty discovers
how deep a hurt can go and how long it takes to heal.
ISBN: 978-0-689-80647-6 (hc.)
[1. Dogs—Fiction. 2. Kindness—Fiction.
3. West Virginia—Fiction.] I. Title.
PZ7.N24Sgg 1996   [Fic]—dc20
95-32558
ISBN 978-0-689-80646-9 (pbk.)
ISBN 978-1-4424-8663-8 (eBook)

0216 OFF

To my granddaughters,
Sophia and Tressa Naylor,
with love

One

After Shiloh come to live with us, two things happened. One started out bad and ended good. The other started out good and . . . Well, let me tell it the way it was.

Most everybody near Friendly, West Virginia, knows how Judd Travers treats his dogs, and how he bought this new little beagle to help him hunt, and how the beagle kept running away from Judd's kicks and curses. Ran to me.

They know the story of how I hid the dog in a pen I made for him up in our woods and named him Shiloh. Judd just calls his dogs cuss words. And everybody in Tyler County, almost, heard how a German shepherd jumped into that pen and tore up Shiloh something awful, and then the secret was out. My dad drove Shiloh over to Doc Murphy, who sewed him up and helped him live.

And then, because my friend David Howard has the biggest mouth from here to Sistersville, most everybody knows how I worked for Judd Travers two weeks to earn that dog. So now he's mine. Mine and Ma's and Dad's and Dara Lynn's and Becky's. We all just love him so's he can hardly stand it sometimes; tail wags so hard you figure it's about to fly off.

Anyway, the thing that started out bad and ended good was that I promised Doc Murphy I'd pay him every cent we owed him for fixing up Shiloh. I looked for bottles and aluminum cans the whole rest of the summer, but only earned two dollars and seventy cents.

When I took it to Doc Murphy, though, so he could subtract it from our bill, he says I can work off the rest, same as I worked for Judd. Next to Judd telling me I can have Shiloh for my own, that was the best news I'd heard in a long time.

And now for the good part that turned bad and then worse: after figuring that everything's okay now between me and Judd Travers—he even gave me a collar for Shiloh—Judd starts drinking.

Not that he didn't drink before. Got a belly on him like a watermelon sticking out over his belt buckle, but now he's drinkin' hard.

First time I know anything about it, I'm coming up the road from Doc Murphy's, Shiloh trottin' along ahead or behind. That dog always finds something old he's got to smell twice or something new he ain't smelled at all, and his legs can hardly get him there fast enough. I think he was down in the creek while I was working at Doc's, and he's trying to make like he was with me the whole time.

I'm following along, thinking how happiness is a wet dog with a full stomach, when I hear this truck coming up the road behind me. I can tell by the sound that it's going faster than it should. My first thought, as I turn my head, is that if it don't slow down, it won't make the bend, and then I see that it's Judd Travers's pickup.

I take this flying leap into the field, like I'm doing a belly flop in Middle Island Creek, and for a couple seconds I can't even breathe—it's knocked the wind right out of me. I watch the truck go off the road a couple feet farther on, then weave back on again, over to the other side, and finally it starts slowing down for the bridge.

Shiloh comes running back, licks my face to see if I'm all right. The question in my mind is did Judd try to run me over or didn't he even see me, he's that drunk? And if Shiloh had been behind me instead of up front, would I be looking at a dead dog right now?

"Judd almost ran me over!" I say that night at supper.

"He *what*?" says Ma.

I tell my folks what happened.

"He do it on purpose?" asks Dara Lynn. Ma's fixed white beans and corn bread, with little chunks of red ham in the beans, and Dara Lynn's counting out the pieces of ham on her plate. Wants to be sure she got as many as Ma gave me.

"I don't know," I tell her.

Ma looks at Dad. "This is serious, Ray."

Dad nods. "I guess I've been hearing right, then. They say Judd's been stopping off at a bar down near Bens Run. Does his drinking nights and weekends."

Ma's anxious. "You'd best keep off the road, Marty," she says. "You, too, Dara Lynn. You hear his truck coming, give him plenty of room."

"All he's going to do is get himself arrested," I say. "Why's he start drinking so hard all of a sudden?" Even I know that when a person does that it means he's bothered.

"Maybe he's thirsty!" says Becky, and we all laugh.

Becky's three. Dara Lynn laughs, too, even though it's something she might have said. Dara Lynn's seven. I'm four years older than that, and supposed to set an example for my sisters, says Ma, which is why it was so hard on my folks when they found out I'd been hiding Judd's dog up in our woods.

"I think Judd drinks because he's unhappy," says Ma. She smooths out the margarine on her piece of corn bread, then takes a real slow bite.

"Maybe he misses Shiloh," says Becky, trying again. I wish she hadn't said that.

"Why?" asks Dara Lynn. "He's got all those other dogs to keep him company."

Ma chews real thoughtful. "I think he looks in the mirror and don't like what he sees," she says. "The fact that his dog kept running away and coming to you, Marty, and the way you kept on working for Judd even though he called you a fool—I think that made him take a good hard look at himself, and it wasn't pretty."

Becky nods her head up and down. "Judd's not pretty," she says, real serious, and we laugh again.

All this time, my dad is breaking up his corn bread over his pile of beans, and then he eats it mixed together, and I notice he's the one not laughing.

"What's worrying me is that Judd's been hunting up in our woods, I think. Rabbits, I expect. I found a beer can up there, the brand Judd drinks, and heard a couple shots yesterday, same as last weekend."

"We've got those woods *posted*!" Ma says, meaning we got signs up around the property saying we don't allow any hunting. But poachers sneak in there sometimes anyway.

Up in our woods, and even in our meadow on the far side of the hill.

Her gray eyes are fixed on Dad now. "Ray, you've got to tell him! I don't want him up there drunk, firing his gun off every which way. One of those bullets could end up down here."

"I'll talk to him," Dad says.

I'm real quiet then. In fact, I'm through with the beans on my plate. Been thinking about taking a second helping, but suddenly I'm not hungry anymore, so I go outside and sit on the steps. It's been real warm and dry for September, and I like to catch a breeze.

Shiloh comes over and lies down beside me, head on my leg. Then he takes this big contented sigh and closes his eyes.

What my folks don't know—what nobody knows except me and Judd Travers—is how the only way I got Judd to let me keep his dog was that I saw him shoot a deer out of season. A doe it was, too. And when he knew I could report him to the game warden—I *would* have, too—he said I could keep Shiloh if I kept my mouth shut about the doe and if I worked for him two solid weeks. I swear Judd must have laid awake nights thinking of the hardest, meanest jobs he had for me to do, but I did 'em, every one.

So a promise is a promise, even if I shouldn't have made it in the first place. There wasn't any point in telling the secret now anyway. The doe and all traces of the killing were long gone.

I lean against the porch post and stroke the top of Shiloh's head, smooth as corn silk. Here I'd thought now that Judd and me were almost, but not quite, friends—you couldn't be *real* friends with a man like Judd Travers—I wouldn't have to worry anymore. But Ma says drink will make a person do things he never in this world thought he'd do, and you put drink in Judd Travers, you got a bomb just waiting to blow up. He might not try to run over Shiloh, or shoot him out of spite, but what if he's up in our woods hunting and Shiloh runs through? What if Judd shoots at the first thing that moves?

After supper Dad comes out, and he's carrying this beer can he found in our woods. He puts it on the front seat of the Jeep, then climbs in and heads down the driveway.

I watch the Jeep pause way out by the road, then turn right and go past the mill. It crosses the rusty bridge to the old Shiloh schoolhouse that's been closed as long as I can remember. After that it's out of sight and I know that in two or three minutes Dad will pull up outside the trailer where Judd Travers lives.

I listen. Yep. About two minutes later, way off in the distance, I hear all Judd's dogs barking at once, which means they hear the Jeep. All those dogs are mean as nails, 'cause the only time Judd don't keep 'em chained is when he takes 'em hunting.

I figure that about this time Judd's looking out his window, wondering who's driving up to see him at seven o'clock on a Sunday night. Then he'll get up and come to the door in his undershirt.

Dad'll walk up the boards that serve as Judd's sidewalk, and they'll stand on Judd's steps awhile, talking about the kind of weather we've been having, and are the apples going to be any good this fall, and when is the county going to fix that big pothole just this side of the bridge.

And finally, after they say all that, Dad'll show Judd the

beer can and say he's sure Judd didn't mean to wander off up in our woods when he was hunting, but Dad figures the beer can is his, and he's been hearing these shots. He surely would appreciate it, he'll say, if Judd wouldn't hunt in our woods. He don't like to make a fuss, but when a man's got children, he's got to look out for them.

My mind can think up about a dozen ways Judd could answer back, none of 'em polite, but I don't let myself dwell on it. I'm running my hand over Shiloh's head real slow, and I can tell by his eyes how he likes it. If Shiloh was a cat, he'd purr.

Becky comes out to sit beside me, and pulls her dress way up to let the cool air fan her belly.

"Shouldn't do that way, Becky," I tell her. You got to start teaching her young or she'll do like that down in Sistersville sometime, not think twice about it.

"Why?" says Becky, smartlike, and pushes her face right up against mine.

"'Cause it's not ladylike to show your underpants, is why," I tell her. I figure that's how Ma would answer.

Dara Lynn's out on the porch now, still eating a handful of cornbread crumbs, and she hears what I say to Becky. I can tell by her eyes she's up to mischief. Wipes her hands on her shorts, then sticks her thumbs down inside the elastic and starts snappin' it hard as she can—*snap, snap, snap*—the elastic on her shorts and underpants both, just to rile me.

Of course Becky laughs and then she's doing it, too, both of 'em snapping away at their underpants in a wild fit of the giggles. Girl children are the strangest people in the world sometimes.

But then I hear the Jeep coming back. Dara Lynn hears

it, too, and stops bein' crazy. Finally Becky gives up and we all watch Dad's Jeep—the one he delivers his mail in—come across the old rusty bridge again, on up the road, then turn in at our driveway.

Ma comes out on the porch, hands resting on her hips.

"Well?" she says, as Dad gets out. "What'd he say?"

Dad don't answer for a moment. Just walks over to the house and throws the beer can in our trash barrel.

"Might be a good idea if the kids didn't play up in the woods for a while," he says.

Ma stares after him as he goes inside.

TWO

Miss Talbot's new to our school this year, and I've got her for sixth grade. She's young, younger than Ma, but she's got the same kind of cheekbones up high on her face. Wears her hair the same, too, pulled back on top and fixed with a barrette, then hanging loose around her shoulders.

David Howard and I sit next to each other. Miss Talbot said we could sit wherever we liked, but it was up to us whether or not she'd let us stay there. Just a polite way of saying that if we cause any trouble, she'll change our seats faster than you can spend a nickel.

Since she didn't know any of our names yet that first day, she asked each of us to tell her something about ourselves, and you wouldn't believe what some of the kids thought to tell.

Sarah Peters told how she fell off a swing last year and broke a tooth. Now who do you figure cares about that? Tooth's been *fixed*! Ain't nothing to see!

Fred Niles said they've got a new baby sister at his house, which wasn't exactly the biggest news in the world, 'cause he's got five sisters already.

Then David Howard told how his family flew to Denver the last week of August, and Denver's called the Mile-High City, because the state capitol's a mile up in the air, only nobody believed him. So Miss Talbot got out the encyclopedia and showed us he was right. Then she told us something else we didn't know: there's a Denver, West Virginia, too. In fact, *two* Denvers, one in Preston County and one in Marshall. Miss Talbot's sister lives in one of 'em, she said.

When it was my turn that day, I told about Shiloh and how I worked two weeks to make him mine, and then Michael Sholt told how there was this drunk man who drove by their house sometimes and once even knocked over their mailbox.

Everyone started whispering then, and the whisper went around the room: ". . . Judd . . . Judd . . . Judd. . . ." it went, one person to the next.

Miss Talbot didn't know who Judd was. Somebody's father, maybe? So she just said she hoped that whoever this person was, he wouldn't get it in his head to drive the next time he was drinking, 'cause he might run over a child or a little dog. And since I was the only one who had told about a dog, she looked right at me, and it didn't make me feel one bit better about leaving Shiloh alone all day.

There's times I wish we could just keep Shiloh in the house while I'm at school. But Ma says when you love someone, you don't keep him locked up, not a dog like Shiloh who likes to run; when you love, you got to take chances.

Every day when school lets out in Sistersville, the bus rolls alongside the Ohio River till it gets to Friendly, then turns and winds up the road toward the little community of Shiloh, which is where I found my dog. Which is why I named him what I did. One by one, sometimes two and three at a time, kids get off. David, of course, gets off in Friendly. Then Sarah and a few of the others, then Michael, then Fred, till at last it's only Dara Lynn and me. The bus goes as far as the old mill and turns around.

And always, there's Shiloh, barreling down the driveway to meet us, his legs can hardly go any faster. Skids sometimes, whole body leanin' sideways, gravel flying out from under his paws, but he's standing there with his tongue out the minute Dara Lynn and me step off that bus, ready to lick us up one side of our faces and down the other.

I love this dog more than I ever loved anything in my whole life, I think. Except Ma and Dad. And Becky. And . . . well, I suppose, even Dara Lynn. One night I dreamed Judd Travers come to me with his shotgun, said he was going to shoot either Shiloh or Dara Lynn, which would it be? And I woke up in a cold sweat—still couldn't decide. Suppose I'd save Dara Lynn, it ever come to that, but boy, she'd have to work the rest of her life tryin' to make it up to me.

I get out the scrap of sandwich I always save in my lunch bucket and make a game of it with Shiloh. Take it out, cupped in my hands, then lie down in the grass, hands under my chest. Shiloh tries every which way to roll me over and get at that crust of bread, little sliver of ham still stuck to it.

After he gets it, though, Dara Lynn has to go through her hugging business, and Shiloh puts up with that, too.

"How's my wittle Shiloh-biloh-wiloh?" she sings, picking him up in her arms like a baby. He washes her face clean with his tongue, 'specially the corners of her mouth where there's still the flavor of lunch.

Too disgusting to watch, you want the truth, so I go on up to the house and Dara Lynn comes after.

On this day Becky's on the porch swing playing airplane or boat, either one. Looks maybe like she's playing boat, 'cause she's got a string hanging down over the side, like she's fishing.

When I get in the house, Ma's on the phone with Dad's sister over in Clarksburg. First time we've had a telephone in three years. Ever since Grandma Preston's mind started to go, Aunt Hettie had to have a nurse come in while she was at work to watch Grandma all the time. It was Dad who paid for that nurse, every spare cent we had.

Last month, though, Grandma Preston had a stroke, and what little sense she had left all but went. Not only that, but her kidneys failed. Got a bad hip so she can't get in and out of bed no more by herself, and Aunt Hettie was up half the night with her, still trying to work days.

"Your mother needs more care than you can give her," the doctor says finally to Aunt Hettie, so Dad drove down, and he and Aunt Hettie put Grandma in a nursing home.

Weird thing is, though, long as we were all trying to care for Grandma Preston ourselves—Aunt Hettie doing the work and Dad sending the money—we didn't get any help. Now that Grandma Preston's in a nursing home, not one penny to her name, the government pays for the nursing home and Dad says we can afford a telephone again and a few other things we've had to do without.

Dara Lynn and I sit down at the table, taking turns

easing our hands into a box of graham crackers and listening to Ma.

"She *did*, Hettie? Oh, land, what next?" Ma's saying.

Becky comes in and we give her a cracker. But soon as Ma's off the phone, I say, "What happened?"

Ma shakes her head. "I want the three of you to promise that I ever get to acting crazy, you'll remember me the way I am now."

Dara Lynn gets this gleam in her eye. "*I'll* remember you acting crazy!" she says.

"What'd Grandma do?" I ask. "How much trouble can she get into when she's in a wheelchair?"

Ma sighs. "She's been wheeling herself into other people's rooms uninvited. *Men's* rooms. She's got it in her head that Grandpa Preston's still alive and they're hiding him somewhere."

Becky stares, but Dara Lynn laughs out loud, and it's all I can do not to grin.

"Aunt Hettie's afraid if Grandma don't behave herself, they'll put her out, but those nurses know what to do. They understand."

Nice thing about a telephone is it helps you make plans. Before, when I wanted to say something to David Howard, I'd have to give the message to Dad, and Dad would tell it to David when he put the mail in their box. Then I'd have to wait all day for Dad to get home to find out what David said.

Now when the phone rings, everybody wants to answer.

Becky, when she gets there first, puts her mouth right up to the phone and says in this tiny little voice, "Hi, I'm Becky and I'm three years old and . . . and I have a dog." Somethin' like that. You almost have to sit on her to wrestle that telephone out of her hand.

The phone rings again and I answer. It's David.

"Why don't you stay at my house Friday night and I'll stay at yours on Saturday?" he says.

I ask Ma. She says yes, if I be sure my socks and underwear are clean.

So Friday of that week, I put my toothbrush in my pencil case before I leave for school, and when Shiloh follows Dara Lynn and me down to the end of the driveway, I'm thinking how when the bus gets back that afternoon, I'm not going to be on it.

I kneel down in the grass beside my dog.

"Listen, Shiloh," I say. "I'm not comin' back tonight. I'm staying over with David Howard, but I'll be home tomorrow, okay?" As though he understands a single word. I'm thinking that maybe he understands something's going to be different, even though he don't know what.

The bus comes then around the bend, and Shiloh barks and backs away. He don't much care for the big yellow monster that gobbles us up weekday mornings, and spits us out again each afternoon.

After I get on and the bus turns around, I always go to the back window and look out. See Shiloh trotting up the driveway, tail between his legs. He stops every so often and looks back, then goes a few steps more.

And I'm thinking that much as I like David Howard, much as I like going to his house, I sure don't like the thought of me being gone a whole night, Shiloh at home without me, and Judd Travers maybe out there in the dark.

Three

Kids are always wild at school on Fridays. Restless to get the weekend started—go poking along the bank of Middle Island Creek, maybe—borrow someone's rowboat and row out to an island, if the water's deep enough. Could wade across, if it isn't.

Funny, but as long as I can remember, Ma's called it "the river." Dad told us, soon as she laid eyes on it after he married her and brought her here, she says, "That's no creek to me; it's wide as a river." So we kids forget sometimes and call it "the river," too.

On the bus going home, Michael Sholt's got another story about Judd Travers getting in a fight down in Bens Run a couple nights back, but I don't hear the end of it, 'cause I get off with David Howard, and Dara Lynn rides the rest of the way without me.

I always feel a little strange at David Howard's. It's a big house, for one thing—all kinds of rooms in it. A whole

15

room just for David. Another room for his father's books and computer. Even a room for plants! I told Ma about that once and she said if it was her house, she'd put some of those plants outside where they belong and make more room for *people*.

Meals are fancier at David Howard's, too. The food doesn't taste any better than it does at home, but Mrs. Howard has placemats under all the plates and cloth napkins rolled up in plastic rings. The way I eat at David Howard's, I watch what everybody else does before I start in.

His folks are nice, though. His dad works for the *Tyler Star–News*, and talks to me a lot about basketball, even though I like baseball better. He always forgets. Asks me about the New York Knicks when it's the White Sox I got my eye on.

Mrs. Howard's a teacher, and she can't help herself: she sees something wrong, she corrects it.

"Shiloh don't like to see me climb on the bus each morning," I say at dinner, about the time she's passing out the dessert.

"He *doesn't*, Marty?" she says. "He *doesn't* like to see you climb on the bus?"

"No, he don't," I answer, my eyes on the chocolate pie, and then David giggles and I know I goofed again.

After dinner, David and me go outside and play kick-the-can with some other kids till after dark, and when we come in, Mr. Howard teaches me some moves on a chessboard. After that we eat some more and watch a video, *Homeward Bound*. Then we take turns in the shower and have to mop up the floor.

That night I'm lying on the top bunk in David's room and I can't believe I'm homesick. Thinking about my family, what they had for supper, whether or not the telephone rang, and who answered. What crazy thing Grandma Preston done this time, and whether Shiloh's watching the door, waiting for me to come home.

I'm thinking Ma will give him extra love tonight. She don't know this, but once—when Shiloh was healing his hurt leg—I woke real early in the morning from where I sleep on our couch, and across the room I saw my ma in the rocking chair. She had Shiloh on her lap, and was rocking and singing to that dog like he was a baby. I figure Ma's just getting herself ready for the day Becky, Dara Lynn, and me are grown and gone.

Haven't heard a peep from David Howard for a while down on that bottom bunk, and I figure he's probably already asleep. We played so hard and so long he's a right to be tired.

I wasn't, though. Hard to sleep with cars going by every few minutes, the beam from their headlights traveling along the wall. I'm lying there on my side, about to close my eyes, when suddenly this horrible face with red eyes and green lips pops right up beside me, not five inches from my own, and bobs up and down—a floating head.

I yell. Can't help myself, and then David's having a laughing fit down below.

"Settle down, you guys," comes Mr. Howard's voice as he passes our door.

I want to know how David did that, though, so I crawl down the ladder and push my way onto David's bed, punching his arm. David's got his head under the covers, he's laughing so hard.

"How'd you do that?" I whisper.

David shows me this rubber Halloween mask. He puts

it on and holds a flashlight under his chin. Then, when he moves around and all that's lit up is the mask, it looks like a floating head. I'm thinking how I can't wait to try that on Dara Lynn.

We lay on our backs on David's bunk and talk some more about school and the story Michael Sholt was telling, about Judd getting in a fight with someone. We talk about the way he's been drinking lately, and I tell him Ma's guess—that Judd looks in the mirror and don't like what he sees.

David raises up on one elbow. I can just make out his face in the dark. His eyes are wide open.

"You know what *that* means!" he says.

"What?"

"He's a vampire!" David says, his eyes about to jump out of his head. Even when David *knows* it's crazy, his imagination still runs off with him.

"You're nuts," I say.

"Vampires *hate* mirrors. If they ever look in a mirror, they die or something."

"Then if he was a vampire he wouldn't even *have* one!" I tell David.

"Oh," David says, and lays back down. A minute goes by and David pops right up again.

"A werewolf!" he says.

"David, you're as crazy as Grandma Preston," I say, and then I'm ashamed. It's not like she *wants* to be.

But David's excited all over again. "It figures, Marty! He looks in the mirror and sees fur and fangs, and he just goes a little crazy. The only way to find out . . ."

I know what's coming before David ever says the next word.

"I'm staying at your place tomorrow night. We'll go check out Judd then. Okay?"

"Okay," I tell him.

David don't think Judd Travers is a werewolf any more than I do. He just likes the idea of spying on him—stirring up a little excitement.

I crawl back up in the top bunk and can hear David snoring after a while. I fall asleep some time later, but don't know how long it's been 'cause all at once, middle of the night, there's this loud yell.

My eyes pop open, and the yell seems to hang in the air like an echo.

Can't figure out where I am. The bed's smooth, not lumpy like our couch. Then I remember I'm at David Howard's, and figure it was me who yelled. Wondered if I'd woke him up.

The dream was so *real*. Dreamed I'd just got up out of bed and walked home. Seemed to be half light—early morning, maybe—and I was hoping Ma would be up, tell me Shiloh was okay. But nobody seemed to be around, and I could see Shiloh sleeping out on the porch.

Whew, I'm thinking. He's all right.

Everything looks calm and natural, but just as I get close to the house, I see this long stick there in the bushes. . . . Looks like a branch has fallen out of a tree, maybe, and then I see it's not a stick at all, it's a gun, and it's pointed straight at Shiloh.

It's the kind of dream where your legs don't move, and you yell and yell, but no sound comes out.

Except I must have made some noise, because next thing I know I hear footsteps out in the hall and our door clicks open.

"Everything okay in here?" comes Mr. Howard's voice, real soft.

"Yeah," I say. "We're okay."

Mr. Howard closes the door again and I look at the clock. Four fifteen. Can't wait for it to turn light so I can go check on my dog.

Four

Dad come by in the Jeep next morning to take me home. Six days a week he picks up the mail in Sistersville for two hundred and eighty families, and after he delivers that, he picks up the mail for three hundred and sixty more outside of Friendly.

We don't go directly home, of course. I got to wait while he stops at every mailbox between David's house and ours. Could've walked it, but I like to open boxes for Dad, stuff the mail in.

What I like most, though, is finding a loaf of banana bread or half an apple pie that folks sometimes leave in their boxes for Dad. People like my dad because he delivers their mail no matter what. Can be seven o'clock in the evening, snowing like you wouldn't believe, but Dad'll be out there in his Jeep, getting that mail through.

Soon as I slide on the seat beside him, though, and we give the mail to David Howard, I ask, "Shiloh okay?"

Dad's moving the Jeep on to the next house. "Looked fine to me this morning," he says. "Why?"

"Just wondering," I tell him.

"You have a good time with David?"

"Sure. I always do."

I'm looking forward to Mrs. Ellison's box, which is coming up soon, because she leaves a piece of cake for Dad almost every day. Sure enough, I reach my hand in her box and pull out a loaf wrapped in foil, and my mouth's watering already. Then I read the label she's put on it: ZUCCHINI BREAD, it says.

"Why'd she have to *ruin* it?" I say. "Who would put squash in a cake loaf?"

Dad just chuckles. "You take a bite of that, you won't even notice," he says, but I figure I can last the morning on the pecan waffles Mrs. Howard made for our breakfast.

I get the mail ready for the next box. "Did you know there are two Denvers in West Virginia?" I say.

"Wouldn't surprise me if there are even a couple more," Dad says.

"How can there be two places named the same in one state?" I ask.

"If you don't incorporate, you can call a place most anything you want," he says. "We could call our own place Denver if we wanted."

"Could we call it New York City or Chicago?"

"Expect you could. Postmaster down in Friendly would have a laughing fit, that's all," says Dad.

After I put the mail in Mrs. Ellison's box and turn up the red flag on the side so she can see she's got mail, I ask, "Dad, what happened at Judd's last Saturday when you went over?"

22

Dad gives a sigh. "Let's just say that Judd wasn't himself, Marty."

"He was drinking again, wasn't he?"

"He'd been drinking some, yes."

"Did he say he'd been hunting up in our woods?"

"Conversation didn't exactly go the way I'd planned."

"So what'd he say?"

"Oh, he rambled on about how you took the best hunting dog he ever had. Just nonsense, Marty."

I can feel my chest tighten, though. It was the one thing I didn't want to hear.

"I earned that dog fair and square!" I say.

"Of course you did. Judd was just jawin' again. But I don't want you and Becky and Dara Lynn up in those woods till I've got this settled. Don't want you up in the meadow either. Next time I hear gunshots, I'm going up there myself and check."

Didn't make me feel any better.

It's nice to be riding along with my dad on a warm September day, though—breeze coming in one window and floating out the other. When we get up as far as our driveway, I decide I'll go on across the bridge with Dad this time and help deliver the mail on the road where Judd lives. Figure this will give Judd a second chance to say something about Shiloh if he's got a grudge building up inside him. Maybe if we can talk it out, things'll be okay.

But when we get up to his trailer, an old brown-and-white thing with rust stains on the roof, Judd's nowhere to be seen. We know he's not out hunting because all three of his dogs are chained. They go crazy when they see the Jeep. Leap and growl and bark, teeth showing, chains jerking.

I put the mail in Judd's box and watch the door, thinking maybe he'll hear all the ruckus and come out. His truck's there. But there's no sign of him, living or dead, and I wonder if he's even fed his dogs this morning.

"Judd don't work Saturdays?" I ask as the Jeep starts up again.

"Think he works every other Saturday, something like that."

"What kind of work does he do?" I try to think what kind of job would be right for a man like Judd Travers. Rattlesnake handler, maybe. Alligator wrestler . . .

"Mechanic," says Dad. "Works on trucks and cars down at Whelan's Garage. I hear he's right good at it."

I guess a man can be good at some things and horrible at others. Good with car and truck engines, and bad with dogs and people.

Dad's route ends a couple miles down at a ford where water comes over the road, and that's where we turn around and head back. After we come across the bridge by the old mill, I take our mail and zucchini bread and head on up to the house, 'cause Dad's got a couple hours of deliveries yet to do.

And here come Shiloh to meet me, legs flying out from under him. I pinch off a piece of the zucchini bread and he gulps it right down. That dog'll eat anything. You give him a piece of bread made of spinach and brussels sprouts, bet he'd gobble that down, too, beg for more.

I go up the driveway beside Shiloh. I'm thinking how he's always in a good mood. Always ready to jump to his feet and do any fool thing you got in mind. Don't matter how tired he is or how hot or cold it is outside, he'll be right there at the door waiting to go with you. You treat a dog right, and he's your friend for life.

Better natured than sisters, that's for sure. Dara Lynn gets up some mornings, looks like she's about to break your arm you even look at her cross-eyed.

I eat lunch—Ma's got some turkey sandwiches waiting—before I head over to Doc Murphy's to do my work.

"What'd you do at David's?" Dara Lynn asks me, mouth full of bread.

"All kinds of stuff," I tell her.

"Did Mrs. Howard have a good dinner?" asks Ma.

I'm only eleven, but I know that when your ma asks about somebody else's cooking, you got to be real careful.

"The chocolate pie was good," I say, and Becky and Dara Lynn both start squealin' about why don't we ever have chocolate pie? "But the rest wasn't anything special," I finish.

"What was it?" Mothers have to know the *details*.

"Some kind of meat, I guess. Some kind of vegetables," I tell her. She don't look so interested after that.

Shiloh follows me down toward Doc Murphy's. Before we get to the end of the driveway, though, I see Judd's pickup coming across the bridge on the right. It gets down at the bottom of our driveway and stops.

Thump . . . thump . . . thump. . . . Hard to tell sometimes if it's your heart beating or your knees knocking, or both of them together. It'd be cowardly to turn around and go back now, so I just keep walking. Shiloh don't, though. He stops dead still.

"Hey, Marty!" Judd opens the truck door and puts one foot out. "Come on down here."

I don't know whether to go or not.

"What you want?" I call.

"Want to show you something."

I don't want much to go, but then Judd gets out and walks around behind his truck. He's pointing to the back, so I go down and walk over.

"Look there," says Judd.

Somebody's taken a nail or screwdriver or something and made a long, deep scratch in the paint all the way from Judd's license plate to the door on the right-hand side.

I give a little whistle.

"You have any idea who might'a done this to my truck?"

Judd Travers is uglier than a snake. Not face-ugly, exactly, but mean-ugly. He ever try being anything but mean, he might not look too bad. Eyes are all bloodshot, though, and his breath—whew! You put your nose down inside a beer bottle, that's his smell.

I shake my head.

He looks at me hard. "You think of any boys who could've done it?"

"Nobody I know."

"Well, you listen around, and if you find out who scratched my truck, you tell me, hear?"

"I'll listen," I say, but I don't promise nothing.

Judd gets in his pickup and drives off, and it's not till he's out of sight that Shiloh comes on down. Don't take a lot to prove that Judd Travers isn't the most popular person in Tyler County.

That man can scare you so bad that even if you haven't done something, you almost wonder if you might. The kind of man you keep imagining all sorts of horrible things happening to, and then you feel guilty you enjoyed it. I'm asking myself if it's such a good idea for David and me to go sneaking around Judd's tonight.

I walk on down to Doc's. He's got an office there in his house, but he don't see patients on Saturdays unless it's an emergency. His wife died ten years ago, and he tries to keep up the grass and flowers, just for her.

Doc figures I owe him about ninety-nine dollars for fixing up Shiloh after he was tore up by the German shepherd. I get three dollars an hour and work three hours every Saturday. Worked two Saturdays so far, so I got nine more to go.

"How's the patient doing?" Doc says, stepping out on the porch when he sees me coming. He's a heavy man, and he grunts some when he reaches down to pet my dog, check where he sewed him up. One of Doc's friends is a veterinarian down in St. Marys, and Doc checked with him after Shiloh was hurt, made sure he was doing right.

"Looks good, Shiloh," he says. "You keep out of trouble, now."

Today Doc wants some bushes transplanted from one side of his yard to another where they'll get more sun. He digs awhile, then I dig. Shiloh just lies on the grass in the shade, smiling at us, mouth open, and we laugh at the way he's watching us work.

"That dog sure has an easy life," Doc Murphy says, stopping to wipe the sweat off his forehead.

I'm wondering what kind of life he would have had if I'd turned him back over to Judd—if Shiloh would even be alive at all, the way Judd used to kick him and starve him every time he run off. Can't help thinking of the three dogs Judd's got left, all chained up, yelping and snarling at one another.

Doc begins digging again, and I hold on to the bush so's

it doesn't fall over while he works at getting the tip of the shovel down under the roots.

"You suppose the rest of Judd's dogs are ruined for good?" I ask. "I mean, once you chain a dog and he turns mean, is he going to be mean forever?"

"That I don't know, Marty," Doc says. "Sometimes I figure there's not all that much difference between a man and an animal. One has two legs, the other four—maybe that's the sum of it. I suppose some dogs and some people are born with meanness in them—something in their bloodline, maybe. . . ." He gives a final grunt, and the dirt ball lifts up. ". . . But a lot fewer than folks believe, I suspect. My own guess is that a little kindness will fix almost anything wrong with man or beast, but I wouldn't swear to it."

I lift the last forsythia bush up out of the ground and carry it over to the hole we dug for it on the other side of Doc's driveway. We work together to set that bush straight. Doc is going to a symphony concert in Wheeling this evening, so I finish the bushes myself, packing in loose dirt in each of the holes, making sure the bush is standing up straight.

Feel like an old man when I'm through, my back so sore. I head home at four, and Ma says I stink. Got to take a bath before David gets here, so I'm smelling sweet as a rose when David's mom drives up to our house. Shiloh never barks at the Howards' car—he's always glad to see David.

"You just have a bath or something?" David says, seeing my hair all slicked down.

"Sweet as a *rose*," I say, drawing out the "o," and I stick my armpit in his face. "Smell."

He laughs and pushes me away.

Ma comes out to talk with Mrs. Howard a few minutes, while David and I take turns on the bag swing we got hanging from our beech tree.

David climbs up the maple close by and sits out on a limb. Then I take the gunnysack hanging by a rope from the beech tree and toss it up to him, high as I can throw. David catches the rope, wraps his legs around the sack stuffed with straw, then slides right off the branch, hanging onto that rope for dear life. Swing swoops down toward the ground and way up in the air on the other side.

"Wheee!" yells David.

I should be having a good time, but I keep thinkin' about what David and me are going to do later.

He don't have any sisters or brothers, so he thinks Dara Lynn and Becky are cute. And they put on such a show of cuteness it almost makes your stomach sick.

Becky's got to sing the ABC song for him, only she always forgets what comes after the "L-M-N-O-P," so she starts all over again. Then Dara Lynn's got to get in the act, and after she shows David Howard all her scabs and bruises, she asks him jokes:

"How do you keep a bull from charging?" she says, grinning.

"I don't know," says David.

"Take away his credit card!" Dara Lynn shrieks.

She don't even know what a credit card is.

At supper, Ma's got apple dumplings for dessert, and we pour milk over them while they're still warm. David runs his finger around the bottom of his dish when he's done to get every last bit.

"What are you two boys planning to do this evening?" Ma asks as she clears the table.

"Fool around outside," I tell her.

I don't have to ask David Howard what he wants to do. David's got it all worked out in his head like a detective story, I can tell. And soon as we close the screen, he turns to me and asks, "How long will it take to get to Judd Travers's?"

Five

I figure when David Howard grows up, he'll be an explorer, a detective, or a spy.

Whenever there's a game where you have to crawl under a bush or slide on your belly or hide in a tree, that's what David wants to play. And because we have a lot more places to hide on our land than he does on his, that's why David Howard likes to come to our house.

Dad's reading Becky a story and Dara Lynn's helping Ma with the dishes. Only reason I got excused was I got a guest, and you can be sure Dara Lynn'll see to it that I have to do 'em two nights in a row.

"Takes about twenty, twenty-five minutes to walk to Judd's from here," I tell David.

"Okay. We'll need a canteen, a map, and a pair of binoculars," says David, his voice low.

"A map?" I say. "David, all we're doing is crossing the bridge and walking along the road till we get to Judd's."

"Not the way *we're* going!" says David. "How are you going to spy on someone if they see you come walking right up the road?"

So to please David Howard, I take the back of a used envelope and make a map of the bridge, the old Shiloh schoolhouse, and the road where Judd lives, plus the small private cemetery back in the trees behind someone's house.

David's brought his own canteen and his ma's field glasses, and I tell him if we don't set off right soon, Dara Lynn'll have all the dishes wiped and be begging to go with us.

We don't have to worry about Shiloh, though. Shiloh trots along beside us as we go down the driveway, but when we turn right instead of left, he pauses, not too sure, then lags ten feet behind us all the way to the bridge.

We stop to look at the pothole in the road. Been there since last spring. Must be seven inches deep, and three feet around.

"Wow!" says David Howard. "Looks like a sinkhole, Marty! I'll bet there's a cave under there, and the roof's falling in."

So of course we have to crawl down the bank and poke around in the weeds and bushes to see if there's a hidden entrance to an unexplored cave that nobody knows about. Every so often you read of someone discovering a new cave. Maybe his foot drops down in it when he's out hiking through a meadow, or his dog falls in and folks hear it whining. If we found a cave here under the road, with passages and waterfalls and stuff, we decide we'd name it the Howard–Preston Caverns.

We waste a good half hour of daylight lookin' for a cave that isn't there, and then climb back up to cross the bridge.

Shiloh won't go, though. Makes this pitiful-sounding whine in his throat. He tucks his tail between his legs and slinks off toward our driveway again. It hurts me to see how scared he still is of Judd Travers. He won't set foot on that bridge for all the rabbits in Tyler County.

"I'll be back, boy," I tell him. If I could just make him understand.

We set off down the road toward Judd's. David stops and takes a drink of water from his canteen, but I can tell he's not even thirsty. Just pretending he is, like we're working so hard and all.

We creep along through the bushes between the road and the creek, darting from tree to tree and waiting till the coast is clear before making a run for the next one. The coast is clear all up and down the road, of course—not a soul outside except an old woman sitting on her porch, and she don't have her glasses on. Don't even see us.

It's fun, though—all the spy talk.

"Agent XRX, Agent XRX. Come in, XRX," says David, holding one fist up to his mouth like a microphone.

"Read you, QZT," I say.

"How close are we now?" asks David.

"'Bout five houses more, I think. It's a brown-and-white trailer."

Problem is the houses are all so far apart up here you can't see Judd's trailer even when it's next one in line. Same as our house.

"Let's cut to the cemetery," says David.

We cross the road, go round behind a house, and creep through a lady's backyard, backs bent while we run like soldiers dodging enemy fire, hills looming up on our left. We pass this little cemetery plot with a low iron fence around it. I mean, it's only two feet high; you can step right over it. There's a whole generation buried there, I guess, and all the names are Donaldson except one.

"Wait!" says David Howard, grabbing my arm.

I stop.

"Which way is the wind blowing?" he says.

"I don't know."

David licks his finger and holds it up in the air. He's still not sure, so he throws a handful of grass up and waits to see how it falls.

"We're going downwind!" he says, his eyes big, like we're on a ship that's sinking or something.

I try to look worried, too. "What do we do now?" I ask. "The dogs might smell us coming." There's no quick way to go around and get to Judd's from the other end, because we got hills on one side, Middle Island Creek on the other.

"We'll just have to be dead quiet," says David. "You want to risk it, XRX?"

"Roger," I tell him.

We get about fifty yards from Judd's trailer and we're down on our bellies, inching along through weeds two-feet high in the field right next to his yard. I'll probably have to explain the grass stains on my T-shirt to Ma, and I sure shouldn't have taken a bath, but it's worth it.

When we get close enough to Judd's trailer we wriggle around toward the road till we can see Judd's front door, and there he is, big as life, sitting out on the steps with a shotgun resting on his knees.

David and I just grab at each other and swallow.

Lucky for us, I guess, that Judd's dogs are chained on the other side, can't see us. They're quiet tonight. I guess when you're a dog, no matter how small your brain is or how full of meanness, you got sense enough to know that when a man's sitting out on his steps with a shotgun across his knees, you don't cause him any trouble.

"You think he's going hunting?" David whispers to me.

"Don't think so," I whisper back.

The scary thing is, Judd don't look like he's going anywhere. Not cleaning his gun either. Just sitting. And once in a while he spits. What's he waiting for? The person who scratched his truck, maybe? Just watching for someone to come along and try it again?

David Howard inches forward again, and I wish he wouldn't. I make my way up beside him and pull him back.

Then we realize Judd's talkin' to himself. Can't make out a single word, just a low kind of mutter. Every so often he slaps a knee or shakes his head, then he's quiet before he starts all over again. Not too hard to see he's been drinking.

It's right about then he suddenly jerks to attention and raises his gun, and I know for a fact I shouldn't be here. Shouldn't be anywhere near this place. But Judd's got his gun aimed at a tree in his front yard. At first I figure this shows just how drunk he is, mistaking a tree for a deer or something, but I raise my head in time to see two squirrels chasing each other around and around that tree trunk.

Judd lifts his gun and aims.

Bang!

One squirrel goes skittering on up the tree half crazy, and the other falls straight down and goes floppin' about the yard.

I can't watch. Put my head down on my arms and pray for that squirrel to die quick. But now all Judd's dogs are going nuts, yelping and barking, and above it all comes Judd's laugh.

"*Gotcha!*" he yells, and I can hear the slap of his hand on his knee again. He don't even stand up to go get the squirrel, or shoot it to put it out of its misery. I look up quick to see the squirrel still squirming, but then it lays still, only its tail twitching.

How can he *do* that way? I'm asking myself. To watch a living thing die slow like that, shot for no good reason at all? Wasn't as though Judd needed it for food—squirrel stew or something—because he don't even get off the step. Just spits again out the side of his mouth.

The other squirrel's comin' back now, probably to see what's happened to his pal, and just as Judd raises his gun again, I yell, "No, don't!" Can't help myself.

David pushes my head down. Judd jerks around.

"Who'zat?" he yells, but his words sound slurred. "Who said that?"

We hear him get up off the steps, and I think my heart's going to pound right through the skin on my chest. I'm about as frightened as I ever been in my life, because David and me weren't just walking down a country road where we've every right to be. We're lyin' belly down on Judd's property, and Judd could put some lead in us quicker than he could spit—say we were trespassing and he thought we'd come to rob him or something.

"Sound like Marty Preston to me," says Judd, and from where I'm lying, my chin on the ground, eyes turned up about as high as I can get 'em, I see Judd looking every which way, trying to figure out where that voice came from. "What you doing over here?" he yells again. "Your dad won't let me hunt on your land, so what you doing on mine?"

I press the side of my head to the ground, my whole

body as flat as it can get. All I can think of is Ma hearing that David and me were found with buckshot in our brains. This has got to be one of the stupidest things I ever did. I can hear Judd's big old boots comin' down the boards stretched across his yard.

Should I say something? I wonder. Call out and tell him we were just goin' by? And then I think how it will look, us just going by Judd's place flat on our bellies. I swallow.

The footsteps stop, don't come any closer. I tip my head so I can look up with one eye, and I see that Judd's so unsteady he's only gone as far as the end of the trailer. Got one hand against it, holding himself up, the other one's got the gun.

"I catch you foolin' around my truck, Marty Preston, I'll blast you to kingdom come!" he yells.

Finally, after the longest two minutes in the world, Judd goes back to the steps of the trailer again and then he goes inside.

David and I lie in the grass not saying a word—not breathing, hardly. Then slowly we inch backward out of those weeds the same way we came in, wondering all the while if Judd's got his shotgun aimed out a window, just watching for the weeds to wiggle.

When we're out of sight at last behind a lilac bush, we make a run for the little cemetery with all the Donaldsons in it, and from there, we cut on back out to the road.

We're breathing too hard to talk, almost.

". . . could of been us. . . ."

"Close as spit. . . ."

". . . squirrel hadn't done anything. . . ."

"Shouldn't have come. . . ."

". . . He knows it was you, Marty. . . ."

Both David and me feel sick inside. But there's one big thought taking up the whole of my mind, now that I seen Judd shoot the squirrel: squirrel season don't start till next month, so Judd's a little early; duck season starts in October; deer season starts in November. . . . But dogs? Not a thing on the charts about dog season. With Judd drinking every evening like he does, I tell myself, and now suspecting me of scratching his truck, he'll make his own rules. There could be a Shiloh season, and it could be any time at all.

Six

I don't sleep so good that night and neither does David Howard. When David comes over to spend the night, Ma opens up our couch to make a double bed, but it's got this bar down the middle inside the mattress, and every so often you hit it with your knee.

Shiloh, though, he sure likes to sleep down at the bottom of that bed. When you wake up in the night but your foot's still sleeping, you know you got a dog on it, that's why.

Both David and me wake early, and lie there talking while the house is still.

"You think we should tell?" David asks me.

"About the squirrel?" I say. He thinks *that's* bad, he should know what I know about Judd Travers.

He nods.

"You could, but it wouldn't do one bit of good. You ever hear of somebody getting fined for shooting a squirrel out of season, when you can walk from here to Friendly and find half a dozen dead on the road?"

It's a whole different thing, killing a squirrel or killing a deer. You can shoot only a few deer a year in West Virginia. During squirrel season, you can shoot six a day! Don't make it any more *right* to shoot a squirrel out of season. Just that the game warden isn't going to drive all the way up here because of a squirrel.

I guess it wasn't the fact that Judd killed a squirrel so much as the *way* he killed it. That's what made us sick. His plain delight in watching it flop about his yard while it's dyin'. What kind of kid was Judd Travers when he was growing up? I wonder. What kind of boy was he when he was fifteen? I'm puzzling over what his ma and dad were like, bringing up a son who could sit there and smile over a small creature's misery.

We must look pretty tired at breakfast, 'cause Ma says, "Were you boys up half the night playing games? You don't look very hungry to me. I don't see that bacon going anywhere."

David and I both reach for a piece of bacon just to show her we're awake and hungry, but we're not. Ma's biscuits are good, though. I show David how to mix a spoonful of honey with a spoonful of margarine—stir it up till it turns creamy, and then spread that on a hot biscuit.

We play on the bag swing till David's dad comes to pick him up. Dara Lynn gets up finally and watches us out the window, but our yelling don't wake Becky. She could sleep with a full brass band by her bed.

The Howards go to the Methodist church, and David's got to go home and change clothes first.

"See you at school Monday," David says as he gets in the car beside his dad.

"How you doing, Marty? You guys have fun?" Mr. Howard calls.

"Yeah," we both tell him. We did, too, but watching a squirrel die before our eyes wasn't part of it.

We like Sundays at our house 'cause they're slow. Dad's home all day, and he'll sit out on the porch swing reading the comics aloud to Dara Lynn and Becky. Takes all the different voices and makes us laugh.

Ma usually listens to Brother Jonas preach on TV, but now she's out in the kitchen making bread. She says that next to her children, she loves baking bread on Sundays about as much as anything she can think of.

She don't say so, but she loves Dad more'n she loves baking bread, too. And this morning after I listen to Dad read the comics, I go back in the kitchen where she's shaping the loaves and she's singing one of the country songs she likes so much:

> "If I could have three wishes,
> I'd spend 'em all on you.
> To love me when I'm lonely,
> To cheer me when I'm blue.
> To laugh with when I'm happy,
> Because I know you're true.
> If I could have three wishes, love,
> I'd spend 'em all on you."

I know it's not me she's singing about. I just smile and Ma smiles back.

I spread out my homework on the table across from her and do my arithmetic problems, trying not to let on that I'm worried:

Multiply: 687   1029   3998
           x .33   x .012   x 7.5
           ─────   ─────   ─────

Divide: 687 by .33   1029 by .012   3998 by 7.5

I wonder if there is ever a time in my whole life that I will have 3998 of something and have to divide it by 7.5. I ask my ma.

"Even if you don't, Marty," she says, "arithmetic helps you think. It helps you learn to solve problems."

I'm thinking arithmetic can't help me solve the kind of problems we've got with Judd Travers. If that was true, I'd stay up to midnight every night just studying that arithmetic book.

The true fact is, I'm wondering if maybe some of Judd's drinking is because of me. The two weeks I'd worked for him during the summer, I'd got to know him some. And after a while we'd talk about his dogs and stuff, so that on the last day, I felt Judd was a little sorry to see me go. Sorry he wouldn't come home from work afternoons and find someone there he could talk to.

I'd figured to go back now and then to visit him— maybe even take Shiloh. But I could never get my dog to set foot over that bridge again, and since I wasn't all that eager to see Judd myself, a good idea just sort of washed away.

After we ate Sunday dinner, though, which at our house is about one in the afternoon, Dad lays down for a nap, Dara Lynn's got her paper dolls out on the swing, Becky's in bed, and Ma's got her feet up, reading a magazine. So I set out for Judd Travers's. I mean to come right out and tell him that yes, I was over there the night before, so he won't think I'm sneakin' around.

This time Judd's working on his truck. Got the hood up, and he's changing the oil. Don't seem like he's been drinking today. Leastwise, he's not drunk yet.

"Hi, Judd," I say.

Judd looks up and goes on tinkering under the hood of his truck. "What you up to?" he asks me.

"Nothin'. Just fooling around the creek," I tell him.

"You takin' good care of my dog?" he says.

Those are the very next words out of his mouth, and what I don't like are the words, "my dog."

"Shiloh's doin' fine," I tell him.

"Thought maybe you'd bring him by one of these days," Judd says. "How come he ain't with you now?"

How do you tell a man that your dog hates him more'n bee stings? "He's home playin' with Becky and Dara Lynn," I say. "They're fixing to spoil him."

Judd just grunts. "You don't take a dog hunting, he'll lose his touch."

"Dad'll probably take Shiloh with him when he starts hunting next month," I say. "Hunting season hasn't started yet, Judd. Only thing you can shoot in West Virginia this time of year is dove."

There's a sly grin pulling back the corners of Judd's mouth. "That a fact?" he says, and spits again as he wipes his hands on a rag.

What I'm trying not to look at is the remains of that squirrel. Pieces of squirrel all over Judd's yard. Looks to me like he got up this morning and threw that squirrel carcass to his dogs. Can just imagine those lean, mean dogs snapping and snarling at one another, eager to get a little blood on their muzzles.

I swallow. "Listen, Judd, I came to tell you somethin'."

"Yeah?" he says.

"David and me—he was over to my house last night—and we were playing spy. That *was* us you heard in your yard."

This time Judd raises up real slow. "So how come you didn't answer?"

"We were scared because you had that gun."

For a moment Judd don't quite know what to say. This amount of truthfulness is almost too much for him to handle. What I haven't counted on, though, is making Judd mad. His eyes get all squinty and the brows come together over the bridge of his nose.

"You expect me to believe that? You come all the way over here to play spy? You weren't *playin'*, boy, you were spyin', and wouldn't surprise me one bit your dad put you up to it."

"He *didn't!* He didn't even know we were here. But we shouldn't have been in your yard, and . . ."

He never even lets me finish. Judd's hollering now: "You and that boy come over here once, you've been here more'n that. And any two boys come sneakin' around my house, won't even answer, got something on their minds besides play. I'm no fool. It was you or that boy, or maybe the both of you, who scratched up my truck, I'm willing to bet, and I catch you over here again, I just may pull that trigger. A man's got a right to protect his property."

"Judd, I . . ."

"Go on home, you hear me?"

Judd's standing there with a wrench in his hand, and his face has gone from plain ugly to pure ugly—not a spark of kindness in those eyes at all.

When I don't move, he yells, "Git!" and takes a step forward, and that's when I turn and head for home.

Oh boy, I've done it now. I kick at a rock just about as hard as I can kick and send it flying into Middle Island Creek. I tell the truth, and look what happens.

Can't believe Judd would really put a bullet in me if he sees me over his way again, but I'm thinking he might could put a bullet in the living thing I love almost more'n anything else in the world. I sure can't go on like this, that much I know.

Dad's working outside when I get home, getting ready to mow. I stand over him as he pours gasoline in the mower.

"Somethin' on your mind?" he asks.

"I wonder if Judd's drinking on account of me," I say, trying to edge in easy on the subject. Dad won't like to hear that David and me were over at Judd's last night any more than Judd did.

Dad looks at me, screws the lid back on the gasoline can, then straightens up. "Now what put an idea like that in your head?"

"I was thinking how after I got Shiloh and worked for Judd, I never went back anymore. I think Judd sort of got used to me being around—somebody for him to talk to."

"Probably so, but I don't think a man starts drinking because an eleven-year-old boy don't show up. Judd's got problems that don't have anything to do with you, Marty. He sure wouldn't get no prize for getting along with people."

"But he says those things about Shiloh—about me taking his dog and all."

"Judd'll jaw on about anything, you give him a chance. You know that. You know and I know and he knows that you earned that dog. Why do you keep worrying about it?"

"I'm afraid he'll get drunk sometime and shoot Shiloh."

"Well, *I'm* worried he'll get drunk, go hunting up in our woods with his rifle, and a stray bullet will hit one of you kids," Dad says. "You want to worry about something real, take that one."

"But after all I did to protect Shiloh—the way that dog come to me—I just couldn't stand it if anything was to happen to him now," I say. I follow Dad as he pushes the mower over to a corner of our yard. "Couldn't we . . . well, invite Judd to dinner or something? Make like we're really friends?"

Dad's looking question marks at me. "Marty, no more'n two months ago, you were hating Judd Travers worse'n a rattlesnake, and now you want to invite him home?"

"Just to keep on his good side." I'm thinking maybe now is the time I should tell Dad I was over at Judd's, but there's something about him that stops me.

Dad rests his hands on the handle of the mower and takes in a big breath. "Fact is," he says, not looking directly at me, "when I was up to see Judd last week, I lost my temper. I'm not proud of it, but it happened. I showed him the beer can, and reminded him our woods and fields are posted, and all he did was cuss me out."

I'm staring. "He *cussed* you?"

"Said I was a sorry kind of neighbor to keep my land all for myself to hunt on. Said if he'd known what a miserly skunk I was, he'd never have let you have that dog at all. In fact, he says that because he *did* give him to you, he could hunt wherever he pleased. That was part of the bargain."

"That's not true!" I yell, my face hot.

"I know it isn't, Marty. Judd was drunk as a coot when he said that, and I should have come home and gone back again when he was sober. But I got a temper, too, when I'm riled. I told him I ever find him hunting on my land, I'm calling the sheriff. That's why I don't want him at our table right now. I'm not *asking* him to stay off my land; I'm *tellin'* him, and I don't want him to think I'm backing down."

I decide not to say anything just then about playin' spy.

Seven

It is sure quiet around our house. Dad never much held a grudge or carried on a quarrel with a neighbor. It bothers him to do it now.

What I don't like is not being able to take Shiloh up to the far meadow to romp and run. We're used to not going up there between Thanksgiving and Christmas when deer season is on, because—signs or no signs—hunters sometimes get in up there and they've got rifles. Shot from a shotgun and bullets from a rifle are different things entirely.

Shiloh can't understand why we've stopped going up to the meadow, though. I come home from school and he gets all excited—does his wiggle dance, front end going left and his rear end going right. Runs right off toward the path to the meadow, yipping for me to come, too. Runs back and forth to show me the way, get me to follow.

"Shiloh! No!" I say.

He just slinks down low, tail between his legs, like he don't know what he's done, but it's bad. Then when I reach down to pet him, he can't make sense of it, I can tell.

He's been running around some with a black Labrador, though, and it's nice to see him have a friend of his own. Those two dogs go off together and sometimes Shiloh's gone all day and half the night. Comes back with burrs and ticks, but eager to be off again the next time his friend comes around.

At school I find out more from Michael Sholt about Judd fighting at Bens Run. Michael says a cousin told him that a friend's uncle had a brother who said Judd owed him some money, and Judd said he didn't. I suppose that by the time a story's passed along to that many people, there's a little added on or a little left out, so I don't know how true it is. But they say Judd had been drinking and he took the first swing. Would have half killed each other if the sheriff hadn't shown up.

I can imagine that all right. Having seen Judd kill two living things now, I can imagine him *half* killing something without no second thoughts whatsoever.

Last week in September Miss Talbot tells us our school is taking part in a project called "Imagine the Future." The idea is to get kids thinking about their lives a little further than what they're going to do over next summer's vacation, she says.

All fifth and sixth graders in a dozen schools are supposed to choose the job they'd most like to have when they're grown. That's just for starters. Then we've got to write a paper on what it would be like to do that kind of work.

Sarah Peters chooses swimmer.

"Swimmer?" I say when she tells me on the bus. "What kind of job is that?"

"Swimming champion," she says.

Sarah took swimming lessons last summer at a camp down near Middlebourne and now she thinks she can go to the Olympics.

I ask David Howard what he's going to choose.

"Biologist, forest ranger, or football player," he says. "Haven't decided yet."

Didn't take me long to think up mine: veterinarian. It's all I can think of that would please me.

When I go to Doc Murphy's that Saturday I tell him what I picked, only I say I'll probably write down "veterinarian technician," 'cause it takes a lot of money to go to veterinary school. He's showing me how to use a soaker hose on his bushes—how to keep moving it every twenty minutes.

"It does take money, and it's real tough to get into veterinary college, Marty," he says, "but there's no harm in aiming high."

I finish watering all the bushes before I go home. David doesn't come over 'cause he's gone camping with his folks. He's decided to write a report on being a forest ranger, and his dad is taking him to visit a real ranger station so he can ask questions and write a good report.

At the supper table, we're talking about Grandma Preston again. Ma called Aunt Hettie over in Clarksburg and, as usual, Grandma Preston was in trouble.

"What's she done now?" asks Dara Lynn, eyes all shiny, can't wait to hear the latest.

Ma starts to tell, then stops: "Dara Lynn Preston, I don't

50

want this told all over second grade," she warns. "This is *family* business."

"I *won't!*" says Dara Lynn.

"Well," says Ma, and then she looks straight at Dad. "Your mother," she says, "has been stealing."

"Stealing?" says Dad.

"The nurse opened the drawer in Grandma's bedside table and found five pairs of eyeglasses. Seems she's been going around from room to room collecting 'em."

Dad gives a loud cough and ducks his head, but you know he's tryin' to hide a chuckle, and we all laugh then. Can't help ourselves.

"She thinks they're hers!" Ma continues. "Says the other patients have been stealing from *her!*"

"I don't never want to get old," says Dara Lynn.

"Well, most old people don't act like that," says Dad. "Grandpa Preston lived almost as long, and he was smart as they come."

"Same with Grandma Slater," says Ma, talkin' about her own ma. "She hadn't gone out picking beans in the rain and got pneumonia, she'd probably be alive yet."

"If she was so smart, how come she was picking beans in the rain?" asks Dara Lynn.

I see Dad cover his mouth, but Ma gets a little testy.

"All of us do things now and then we shouldn't," she says.

"That's the truth," says Dad.

It's right about then the phone rings, and because Becky's just slid from her chair, ready to go out and play, she grabs it and answers.

"Hi!" she says. She's holding the mouthpiece right under her nose. "My grandma . . ." she begins.

"Becky!" yells Dara Lynn.

"Get that phone away from her, Marty," says Ma.

I'm already reaching around for it, but Becky's turned her back to me and is facing the wall, her tight little fists closed around that telephone.

"Hi," she says again. "What's your name?"

And then I hear his voice: Judd Travers.

"You turn that phone over to your daddy!" he says.

I am trying to wrestle the phone away from her, and Becky is screeching at the top of her lungs. She stops long enough to ask, "What's your *name?*" again, then screeches some more.

"You never mind my name!" We can hear Judd's voice over the whole kitchen. "Give that phone to your daddy, like I said!"

Dad's on his feet now. He's removing the fingers of Becky's right hand from the telephone, one by one, and I'm removing the fingers of her left. Becky gives a final squeal, enough to make your ears sing, and goes out on the porch bawling. Screen slams after her.

"Hello?" says Dad.

The rest of us wait.

"Ray Preston, I come home this evening to find my mailbox pushed flat over on the ground. Not a scratch on it, so I know no car backed into it by mistake. I'm saying I think your boy was over here today and knocked over my box. Maybe him and that kid from Friendly."

I stare openmouthed at my dad.

"What makes you think Marty had anything to do with it?" asks Dad.

"Because somebody scratched up my truck a week or two back, and I'm thinking it's Marty who done it. I want

52

him over here tomorrow digging me a new hole, and I want that post set in cement."

"If Marty did it, you can be sure I'll have him put it up, but hold on while I talk to him," says Dad. He turns to me.

"I didn't do it, Dad! I didn't scratch up his truck, neither!"

"Sure of that, son?"

"Yes, I'm sure!"

"You know who did?"

"No."

Dad studies me a moment, then puts the phone back to his ear. "He says he didn't do it, Judd."

"You believe a kid who'd come over here hiding on my property, spying on me, then saying he don't know nothing about my mailbox?" Judd is shouting now. "What's he over here for, then? He and that kid from Friendly? You ask him that."

"Look. I'll talk to him, Judd. If he did it, we'll both come over and put that box to rights. But I think you've got the wrong boy. It just might be, you know, that since you've knocked down a few boxes of your own lately, the way you've been driving, someone's trying to settle the score. I'm just guessing."

"Well, I'm guessing your kid, and until he puts up my box, you've got yourself some trouble," says Judd. And hangs up.

Ma and Dara Lynn are staring first at Dad, then at me. Even Becky's stopped her squalling and is standing outside the door, nose pressed flat against the screen, 'fraid she'll miss something.

"Marty, let's you and me go outside and have a talk," Dad says.

Boy, I want this talk about as much as I want poison ivy on the roof of my mouth. But Ma brings Becky in, we go out, and we sit on the porch swing on this cool September night, one square of yellow from the window shining on the floorboards.

"That true what Judd says—that you and David were over there on his property, spying on him?"

"We were just playing," I say. Even my voice sounds guilty.

"What did you do?"

"We were crawling along in the grass—making like spies. David wanted to see what Judd does at night."

"What does he *think* he does at night?"

I'm looking down at my hands, rubbing my two thumbnails together. It's so silly it's embarrassing. I shrug. "See if he turns into a werewolf or something."

The swing jiggles slightly as Dad half turns and stares at me.

"Judd was sitting on his steps with a shotgun, and we saw him shoot a squirrel," I go on. "When he started to shoot another one, I yelled, 'No, don't!' Couldn't help myself. But David pushed my head down and we stayed hid that way. Judd tried to find us there in the weeds, but he was too drunk."

This long, long sigh comes out of my dad—almost like it's got no end to it. He sounds plain tired. Worn down.

"If you tried, you couldn't have picked a worse time to do something like this," he says. And then, "Marty, *did* you have anything to do with Judd's mailbox, or scratching up his truck?"

"No! I already told you!"

"But how do I know you're telling the truth? Because

you say so?" He's looking at me there in the dim light, and I'm remembering how I kept Shiloh secret from him when the dog first come to me. Thinking how I'd told Dad I hadn't seen Judd's dog in our yard when he asked, not mentioning I'd seen it up in our woods. Not for one moment letting on that I *had* him up there.

"You lied once, you know."

"I know. I lied then, but I'm not lying now."

"So, I've got to decide whether what you're saying now is the truth," says Dad.

Neither of us is pushing the swing. I can see Dara Lynn's shadow just inside the door, standing close as she can get to hear what we're saying.

"What we've got here," Dad goes on, "is a man who's drinking heavy, doing things when he's drunk he don't even remember, and getting ready for hunting season, if he hasn't started shooting already. Until I give the word, I don't want you so much as crossing that bridge. I want you as far away from Judd Travers as you can get. I've got enough problems on my hands without you making more. You got that understood?"

"Yes," I tell him.

Dad gets up from the swing and starts inside.

"Dad?" I say.

He stops.

"I didn't mess around with his truck or mailbox. If there's some way to make you believe that, just tell me."

"Keep out of trouble," Dad says. "That's all I ask."

Eight

Sunday we're restless. Shiloh's tried four times to lure me up to the far meadow where he runs himself in circles, and each time I say, "No, Shiloh!" He's confused. We all hear a gun go off somewhere that afternoon. Don't think it's in our woods, but we can't be sure.

Even Dara Lynn's got an ache to go up there, 'fraid as she is of snakes. Last summer you couldn't lure her there with ten ice-cream sundaes. But today there's something in the air tells us fall is coming. The wind'll get cold, and the path to the meadow will be ice all the way up. If we don't go soon, we'll lose our chance. But we can't, and that's why we've got the jumps.

It's just after Sunday supper, still light in the sky. Becky's getting cranky, and Dara Lynn's pestering me to play hide-and-seek with her. I'm hanging on the bag swing, listless like, twirling myself around and around and letting one toe of my sneaker drag the dirt. Ma and Dad are inside

56

listening to some man on TV who wants to be the next governor of West Virginia.

"Who we going to play hide-and-seek with?" I ask her. "You hide and then I hide and then you hide . . . where's the fun in that?"

"Becky can play," Dara Lynn says.

"Yeah!" yells Becky. "Let me play, Marty! And Shiloh can play!"

Shiloh hears his name and pads over, ready for something, he don't know what. Why wasn't I born into a family of nine boys? I'm thinking. A baseball team! I think of my ma being one of nine children, and how they must never have lacked for something to do, someone to do it with.

The swing keeps turning around and when I face forward again, there's Dara Lynn and Becky and Shiloh, all lined up looking at me with begging eyes.

"Okay," I say. "I'm 'it.' You two go hide."

I lean my forehead against the rope as the swing goes on its lazy circle around and around. "Five . . . ten . . . fifteen . . . twenty. . . ." I say.

"*Hide*, Becky!" I hear Dara Lynn screech.

I get to a hundred and still hear Becky running around up on the porch. Count to two hundred.

"Here I come, ready or not!" I yell, and open my eyes.

Becky's on a chair on the porch, got a pillow over her, feet sticking out. I smile and play like I don't see her. Go after Dara Lynn instead.

I'm looking around in back of the chicken coop, the shed, but all this time she's behind one of the tires on Dad's Jeep. I get just far enough away from that bag swing, and in she comes, her skinny legs flying. That girl can run!

"Free!" she yells, pounding one hand on the bag swing. Becky slides down off the porch chair and I make like I'm trying to beat her to the swing. I let her pound her little hand on it.

"Fwee!" she sings out.

"Okay, I got to be 'it' again," I say, and drape one leg over the swing, circling around, my eyes closed. "Five . . . ten . . . fifteen. . . ."

Out of the corner of my eye I can see Becky starting up the path to the far meadow. "Don't you go up there, Becky!" I call.

She stops and turns around. I bury my head again and go on counting.

Then Dara Lynn stubs her toe—Ma *tells* her not to go barefoot—and she's howling like she broke a leg.

I get up off the swing again—Becky's sitting down now on the path—and go see whether Dara Lynn's going to live or die.

Ma comes to the door with her scolding look.

"We're *trying* to hear what this man has to say!" she says, and I tell her I can handle it, so she goes back to the TV.

I get Dara Lynn to sit down on a stump and take a good look at her toe. She's dislocated it, is what she's done, 'cause the end part sort of hangs loose, bent to one side. Happened to me once—twice, I think—so I know. Dara Lynn looks down at it, too, and then she's howling again.

"Dara Lynn, shut up," I tell her. "If you stop yelling for one minute, I'll fix it."

She stops, but she's got her mouth open, ready to let loose with the next.

"This is going to hurt for two seconds and then it'll be okay," I say.

She's crying now, shaking her head and holding her foot.

"You got a choice," I say. "Either you let me put your toe back in place—it'll hurt for two seconds—or you go to Doc Murphy. Which you want it to be?"

Dara Lynn scrunches up her face something fierce, closes her eyes, and tips her head back so she can't peek. "Fix it," she says.

I hold her foot in my hand, then gently take hold of the end of her bent toe and give it a little tug.

Dara Lynn yelps and jerks her foot, but when she looks down again, the toe's back in place. Maybe I *should* think of becoming a vet, not just a helper.

"Okay," she sniffles. "You got to count to three hundred this time, though, 'cause I have to run slower, and I got the perfect hiding place."

I sit down on the swing again and count to three hundred. "Five . . . ten . . . fifteen . . . twenty. . . ."

When I go out hunting for the girls again, Dara Lynn's got a good hiding place all right—inside Dad's Jeep—but it's too hard to get out of in a hurry, and I beat her back to the swing.

Then I go looking for Becky. Look behind the bushes, under the steps, on the porch.

"Allee, allee in come free!" I yell after a while. "You're home free, Becky. Come on in."

But nothing happens.

"Becky?" I call.

Dara Lynn joins the search. But Becky's gone.

Nine

It's when I remember I last saw Becky sitting on the path to the far meadow that my legs like to give out.

"Becky!" I yell again.

Dad comes to the screen. "What's the matter, Marty?"

"We can't find Becky," I say. "We were playing hide-and-seek and I can't find her."

He comes out on the porch. Then Ma.

"What?" says Ma. Her face looks all pulled around the edges.

I tell it again.

"Where did you *see* her last?" asks Ma, hurrying down the steps.

"Up on the path." I point to the steep dirt trail that leads to the woods and the far meadow. "I told her not to go up there, and she sat down. Then Dara Lynn hurt her toe, and I don't remember if I saw Becky after that."

Ma's running now, heading for the path. The sky's got that in-between look. Isn't day, isn't evening. Everything looks in sharp focus, but you know it's not for long.

"Where's Shiloh?" Ma calls over her shoulder. "If Becky wandered off, how come he didn't go with her?"

Shiloh is stretched out on the ground between the house and the shed, just enjoying himself.

"Why isn't he *with* her?" Ma cries again, and she looks with such anger at my dog it scares me. "What good is he if he can't protect Becky?"

"Ma . . . !" I say.

Then she turns on me. "You should've *watched* her!"

"Get the flashlight, son," says Dad. "Dara Lynn, you go in the house in case she shows up there. Don't let her wander off again."

I tear into the house and grab the flashlight from off the top of the refrigerator, then run back out. Shiloh sees all the excitement now, and he's up on his feet, ready to join in.

I feel empty and rattly, like all my ribs are knocking together. How much should you expect from a dog, after all? How does he know where Becky's supposed to go and where she isn't? He's only been with us a month or so.

"Becky?" Ma's yelling into the bushes on either side of her, and I follow her up the hill.

"Becky!" yells Dad. "Where are you? Yell so we can hear you."

Somewhere far off I hear a gun again. At least I think it's a gun. Could have been a firecracker, I suppose. It's hard to tell sometimes. I look at Dad, though, and he heard it, too. It's a gun. I can tell by his face.

We get to the fork in the path. Go left, you end up in

woods, up near where I hid Shiloh—where I built his pen. Go right, you'll come to the meadow where I'd run him sometimes, nobody could see us from below.

"Marty," says Dad, "you just sit right here and keep your eye on the yard. What I don't want to happen is for Becky to wander back home, think we're all gone, and go off again."

"O-Okay," I say, and hand over the flashlight to him. He heads for the woods, Ma takes the meadow, and I sit down on the big flat rock at the fork where David and I used to play spaceship sometimes.

I don't sit down so much as I sink. I just got a thought so terrible that it makes my knees give out in earnest.

What if Judd Travers is up here hunting deer with a light? Some hunters do that way, which is about the lowest way you can hunt a deer—stun it with a powerful light and when it stops dead still in front of you, shoot it with a rifle.

But that's not the terrible thought, that's just for starters. What if, because I didn't report Judd to the game warden when he killed that doe out of season, he feels he can get away with it again? If I'd reported him, maybe they would have taken away his license or something. But because I wanted Shiloh so bad, I didn't say nothing. And maybe saying nothing is why Becky's missing now. Maybe one of those stray bullets found her, and I traded Becky for Shiloh.

I bend over, hugging my stomach, like I got belly cramps. So scared my arms are shaking. How can you think you're doing the right thing, and it's maybe not right at all?

Down below in the yard, I can see Shiloh standing up, looking around. I'd thought he'd follow us up here, been wanting so bad to come. Guess when you scold a dog four times in one day, he learns a little something. But why couldn't he have learned to stick with Becky? Why wouldn't he just naturally know that Becky, being the smallest, needed him most?

"Becky! Becky!" I can hear my ma yell.

There's no answer.

It's going to get dark right soon, now. It's already black back in the trees. I can see the spot of yellow from Dad's flashlight from time to time, then it disappears again.

Ten minutes go by. Which is worse, I'm thinking—sitting here waiting for Becky, or lying in the weeds beside David Howard when Judd was yelling, "Who's there?" and was starting over with his gun to find us?

I think I'd choose to be back there and take my chances at Judd's. At least what was happening, or going to happen, would take place before my eyes. Here I don't know. All I can do is sit.

Dad's coming back through the trees now, then I hear Ma's footsteps not far behind.

"I'm calling the sheriff, ask for a search party," Dad says, and I hear a tremble in his voice. Ma's starting to cry.

We make our way down the steep path, and Dad's talking out loud. Praying, I guess he is, closest he comes to prayer: "I wish to God I hadn't riled Judd; wish to God I'd handled that better."

I can see right off I'm not the only one feeling responsible. Guess I'd thought that when you get to be thirty-eight, like Dad, you don't have these questions. You just *know*. Now I'm seeing the other side of things.

"Ray," Ma sobs, her nose all clogged up. "You don't think Judd would come through those woods and just *take* Becky, do you?"

"No, not even drunk. I don't think so." Dad puts an arm

around Ma to steady her, but his voice gives him away. Needs a little steadying himself.

Shiloh's standing down at the bottom of the path waiting for us, tail wagging, tongue hanging out, glad to see us coming back.

But Dad's not glad to see him. In fact, seems to me that Dad's right foot sort of reaches out and gives that dog a push. Not blaming Shiloh, exactly, but not feeling so kindly toward him, neither.

Dara Lynn's standing at the screen door bawling 'cause she don't like being left in the house by herself at night, and nobody's paying her much mind. Dad steps up on the porch and goes straight for the telephone. Ma's telling Dara Lynn to hush.

I go up on the porch and wait for Shiloh to follow us in, the way he does when we're all on the porch in the evening. But he just trots back down the steps, goes over to the shed, and stands there wagging his tail.

And suddenly my heart begins to beat faster. I leap off that porch, not even bothering with the steps, and open the door of the toolshed a little wider.

There's Becky, sprawled out on the dirt floor, head on a bag of chicken feed, her lips letting out little fluttery sounds while she sleeps.

I'm so happy I shout. Then I hug Shiloh and get the wettest kiss this side the Mississippi. I shout once more. The shout don't even wake Becky up. Her body jolts for a second, then drops right back into sleep.

But now Ma is coming out of the house, then Dara Lynn and Dad.

"I found her!" I yell. "Shiloh was looking out for her all the time. Led me right over to the shed."

64

Everyone comes running, and I can't tell who's hugging who. Ma's hugging Becky, Dad's hugging Ma, Dara Lynn's hugging Shiloh, but I'm not hugging Dara Lynn. Not that far gone. I guess I'm hugging Shiloh, too.

Dad picks up Becky in his arms and carries her into the house and she don't even open her eyes. Bet you could operate on her brain and she wouldn't even feel it.

Ma takes off Becky's shoes and lays her down on her bed, clothes and all, and then the only thing left to do is have some ice cream. Dad calls the sheriff again to tell him the search is off, and Ma's dishing up big helpings of fudge ripple. Shiloh gets the first dish.

"Would have saved us a lot of grief and worry if that dog could talk," says Dad. He's smiling now.

"He did talk, we just didn't ask the right questions," I say. "He knew Becky was in that shed the whole time. She must have gone in there to hide and fell asleep. He was watching over her, not making any fuss. It was when we all went in the house without her that he figured he ought to let us know."

"Well, if I don't see Judd before next weekend, I'm going over there and settle this whole thing peaceably," Dad says. "Can't go on worrying this way every time a gun or firecracker goes off."

I sleep real good that night.

Ten

The *Tyler Star–News* says that rabies has been reported in Tyler County, and Dad says it's time we took Shiloh to a vet, make sure he has all his shots.

We know for a fact that Judd never takes his dogs to a vet unless he has to. Says with his dogs being chained and all, how are they going to get rabies?

Judd'll do most anything to keep from spending a nickel he don't have to, but Ma says if he took the money he spent on beer and spent it on his dogs instead, he'd have a lot happier, healthier animals. Happy and healthy ain't what interests Judd, though. Hunting is.

Doc Murphy gives us the name of his veterinarian friend down in St. Marys, and we make an appointment for Tuesday afternoon late. Dad goes to work early that morning to get his mail delivered in time, and about four o'clock, after Dara Lynn and me get home—have some pop and cheese crackers—Dad and Dara Lynn and me put Shiloh in the Jeep and drive to the vet's.

John Collins is his name and, just like Doc Murphy, he uses part of his house for his clinic. Shiloh is not one tiny bit happy about going, let me tell you. He's happy about gettin' in the Jeep, though, and likes to ride up front with Dad, his head out, the wind blowing his ears. Dara Lynn and me laugh at the way spit drops off the end of his tongue. Jeep gets going fast enough and the wind'll blow that spit right into the backseat. Dara Lynn lets out a shriek when some of it smacks her arm.

Once we get to the clinic, Shiloh knows something is up. Don't know how dogs can tell that, but they seem to. Not a place he's ever been before, that's one thing. The scent of other dogs around, that's another. Scared dogs, too.

We're walking up the sidewalk with Shiloh on a leash, and the more he smells the bushes, the more scared he gets. By the time we reach the door, his tail's so far tucked in between his legs he can hardly walk. Dara Lynn picks him up in her arms and carts him inside.

Dad signs in at the desk, and a young woman in a blue shirt rubs Shiloh on the head, but that don't fool him one minute. He knows right off this is a place he don't want to be. Knows it for sure when a fifteen-pound cat reaches out and swats at him as we go past.

We sit in a row on the plastic chairs and Shiloh's sitting on the floor between my feet. I sort of press the calves of my legs close around him like a hug, but I can feel him shaking. I reach down and pat Shiloh on the head. He licks my hand, but it's not a very strong lick. Think he's saying, "I thought you liked me. How come you're bringing me here?"

Dad's reading some pamphlets on distemper, rabies, and something called hepatitis. I'm looking at a dog chart over on the wall. Shows a side view of a dog, and every part of him is named—parts of a dog I never even heard of before. Figure if I'm going to be a vet I got to know them all, so I start memorizing 'em right here—the hock joint, loin, croup, withers, brisket, stifle, flews. . . . Should've brought my notebook, I'm thinking, so I could put it all down.

Dara Lynn, though, is reading about worms. She sits there with her mouth full open, eyes big as quarters, and nudges me in the side.

"Marty," she whispers, "you know that puppies have *worms* in 'em?"

"Yeah," I tell her. "I know dogs can get worms."

"*Live* ones!" says Dara Lynn, eyes like fifty-cent pieces now. "Crawling around *inside* 'em!" She's looking more horrified every minute. Then she looks over at me. "Maybe Shiloh's got 'em."

"I suppose he could have."

"How would they know?" she asks me.

I lean over and whisper: "You have to look in his poop."

"EEeeuu!" Dara Lynn cries, and claps her hands over her mouth.

Only thing I like better than teasing Dara Lynn is making her sick.

Now it's our turn to take Shiloh into an examining room. I get up and tug on the leash, and Shiloh follows, looking about as mournful as a dog can look.

The vet is a tall man—must be six feet four, I'll bet—and he's got on a blue shirt, too. Got a big head, big ears, and a big smile.

"Well, well, so this is Shiloh!" he says in a friendly, calm kind of voice as Dad lifts our dog up and puts him on the examining table. "This the one Doc Murphy told me about?"

"He's the one," says Dad.

The first five minutes all John Collins does is pet Shiloh and talk real soft. Runs his hands behind his ears, smooths his head, and pretty soon Shiloh's feeling like maybe this isn't going to be so bad. Starts frisking up a little, tail begins to wag, and then he's lickin' John Collins all over his hands and chin. The vet laughs.

He asks us questions about Shiloh, about how many shots he's had, and of course we don't know the answers because we don't know who had him before Judd. Wants to know what we feed him, and I can tell he don't like the idea of table scraps.

"You've been taking real good care of him, but he'd be even healthier if he had more protein in his diet," John Collins says, and tells us what kind of dog food we should be buying and where we can get it cheapest.

Then he gives Shiloh a couple of shots—Shiloh's right good about it, just flinches a little—and tells us never to give him bones, make sure he has fresh water, clean his food dish every day, what to do for fleas. . . .

When Dad and Dara Lynn take Shiloh out to the desk to pay the bill, I say to John Collins, "Something I've been thinking on: Chaining dogs makes 'em mean, don't it?"

"It makes them scared, so they act mean," the vet says. "When you chain a dog, he feels trapped. If other dogs or people come over and he thinks he might be attacked, he tries to pretend he's big and fierce in order to scare them off."

"And these dogs just stay mean for life?" I ask.

John Collins shakes his head. "They don't have to. Once you unchain a dog, he doesn't feel so threatened. Knows he can get away if he has to. He may not settle down right then, but if he learns to trust you, knows you'll treat him right, he can become a loyal, gentle dog."

We go home and I sit at the kitchen table and write all that down for my report. We got a vet now; I can call him and ask questions, and I'm thinking how maybe some day I'*ll* have an animal clinic—my name there on the door. Folks will bring their pets in with all kinds of problems, and I'll know just what to do. But two days later, something happened and I sure didn't know what to do then.

It's after school on Wednesday—a common kind of school day. Couple kids give their reports for their "Imagine the Future" project.

Sarah Peters stands up and reads how she is going to be a swimmer and swim the English Channel. Miss Talbot says that's an interesting goal, but what about the rest of her life? She has to be thinking about what else she could do with swimming even after she becomes a champion.

Sarah turns her paper in, and Fred Niles reads the report he's written. He wants to be a policeman, and if he can't get on the police force, then he'll settle for rescue squad.

Miss Talbot says this is a good example of how you can use your desire to help and protect people in several different ways. The boys all give Sarah our smart look, but then Laura Herndon gets up and says she wants to own a restaurant. If she can't own her own restaurant, she says, she'd like to be a cook. If she can't be a cook, she'll be a waitress. And if she can't get a waitress job, she'll start out as a dishwasher and work her way up. Boy, Laura sure knows how to please a teacher. Miss Talbot likes Laura saying how she's willing to start out small and work up.

David Howard and I look at each other and figure

maybe we better do a little more work on our reports before we give them.

It's about five o'clock that afternoon that something happens.

Dad's not home yet. Ma's in the kitchen cooking some turnips and onions, and listening to the news.

Dara Lynn has a wire strung between the chicken coop and the shed, and she's got these little cereal boxes fastened to it like cable cars or something, and she's running 'em back and forth. Sort of neat, really. Wish I'd thought of it myself.

Becky's rolling around in the grass with Shiloh, who's looking about as bored as a dog can look and still be polite about it. Becky rolls over his back and then rolls the other way. Each time Shiloh sort of braces himself, digging his paws in. Don't even protest. Just turns around and licks her now and then.

I'm trying to pick enough apples off our two apple trees to see if there's enough for Ma to make applesauce. The peaches are all gone now, but Ma wants every last apple I can find.

I've found about six, when I hear this barking and carrying on. Sounds like it's far away but coming closer. Shiloh turns his head in the direction of the sound and stands up, body all tense, and Becky rolls right off in the grass.

"Who's that? Your friend?" I ask Shiloh, thinking of the black Lab.

But the noise is too much for a single dog. Gets louder and louder, and I'm wondering what it could be when suddenly, here come these three dogs through the trees back beyond the house. I know the minute I see them that they belong to Judd Travers.

Eleven

There's not even time to think. I grab Shiloh up in one arm, Becky in the other, and run up on the porch.

"Ma!" I yell, and she's already halfway to the screen. She opens it for me and I drop the two inside. Shiloh runs over to a window and stands up on his hind legs, front paws on the sill, wanting to see.

"Dara Lynn?" calls Ma.

I turn around on the porch to see Dara Lynn backed up against the chicken coop, like her body's frozen, dogs all around her snappin' and snarlin', and first thought in my head is that Judd's sicced 'em on us.

Ma goes charging down the steps and grabs the clothes pole that props the line up on wash day. I grab my baseball bat from off the porch and we're running over to that chicken coop.

Dara Lynn's screamin' now, elbows up over her face, and

72

this one dog, the black-and-white one, lunges forward and nips her arm.

Whack! Ma brings down the clothes prop on the black-and-white dog. The others snarl and turn our way, but I'm swinging that bat out in front of me ninety miles an hour and Ma's bringin' that clothes prop down a second time. The dogs back off.

Air is filled with noise. Dogs are yelping, Ma is shouting, Dara Lynn's screaming, Shiloh's yipping, Becky's standing at the screen squalling, and the hens are all carrying on in the chicken coop.

The black-and-white dog seems to be the leader. As Ma's pole comes down again he hightails it out of the yard, and the others follow.

Ma grabs Dara Lynn and rushes her in the house, cleans that bite with soap and water.

About this time Dad comes home.

"Whose dogs are those running up the road?" he asks.

"Judd's!" I tell him. "They got loose and come over here, and one of 'em bit Dara Lynn."

She's sobbing. "I didn't do nothing! All I was doing was playing out in the yard and those dogs come up and bit me."

"You sure they were Judd's?" Dad asks.

"I'd know 'em anywhere," I tell him.

Ma calls Doc Murphy and he says to call the sheriff and get those dogs picked up. The one that bit Dara Lynn'll have to be kept locked up for ten days to see whether or not he's got rabies. If he does, Dara Lynn's got to have shots. If we can't find the dog, she'll have to have 'em anyway.

Dara Lynn howls again.

Dad calls the sheriff and he says someone already

reported them, that those dogs killed somebody's cat. He's got a man out looking for them.

Dara Lynn's sobbing now and Becky squalls, too, just to join in. Shiloh runs from window to window, whining, standin' up on his hind legs. Meanwhile Ma's turnips have boiled dry and the pan's starting to scorch.

Ma turns off the fire, takes Becky out on the swing, and tries to cool her own self down.

"Let's just sit out here a spell and rest," she says. "Becky, it wasn't you got bit, so quit squallin'. Dara Lynn, you're not going to die anytime soon, so just come sit here by me. Let me have five minutes of peace and quiet or my head is going to fly straight off."

Becky looks up at Ma's head and starts suckin' her thumb.

Dad and I come out on the porch then with Shiloh, and we sit on the steps while Shiloh goes trotting all around the yard, smelling for a trace of those dogs. Guess a dog's nose tells him a whole lot we don't know anything about.

"Wonder how in the world those dogs got loose," Dad says. "Judd had chains on 'em that would have held a grown man. Were they dragging their chains, Marty, or what? I didn't notice."

"No. Looked to me like they were all unhooked at the collar," I tell him.

And just when we thought we'd had about enough excitement to last us a while, here come Judd's pickup turning into our drive.

"Well, look who's comin'," says Dad.

Shiloh stands so still it's like he's turned to stone. He knows the sound of that pickup better'n he knows his own name, almost. And soon as it stops beside Dad's Jeep and

Judd puts one foot out, Shiloh races over to our steps and crawls underneath. Seem like he don't even trust that I can save him. Got to get to some deep dark place away from the reach of Judd Travers.

Judd comes stompin' across the yard in his cowboy boots, and his face looks like thunder. If you was to give Becky her crayons and tell her to draw it, she'd choose purple.

"Ray Preston, I accuse you of turning my dogs loose," Judd says right off, a voice three times too loud.

"Now calm down, Judd. I did no such thing," Dad tells him.

"You put your boy up to it, then."

"Marty didn't have anything to do with it."

"Well, somebody come by and unhooked the chains on all three of 'em, and a neighbor says he saw my dogs coming off your property."

Now Ma speaks up: "They were here all right, and one of 'em bit my daughter. Show him, Dara Lynn!"

Dara Lynn holds up her arm and gives a loud sniffle.

"If Marty hadn't got Becky, no telling what they might have done to *her*," Ma continues.

But Judd don't believe it.

"That is a put-up lie, I ever heard one. Sheriff tells me he finds my dogs, he's keepin' the one in a cage for two weeks. That's my second-best hunting dog, the black-and-white."

"It's the only way they can tell for sure whether or not the dog has rabies," Dad says. "Any dog that bites someone has to be watched."

"I see what you're up to, don't think I don't!" Judd goes on, like he never heard one word. "You took my best hunting dog and now you're cooking up some story about my second-best. I'm going to lose two good weeks of hunting because of this, and I want you to loan me that beagle. I can use him."

My heart almost explodes inside my chest.

"No!" I say.

"Judd," says Dad, "why don't you sit down? We can talk this over man-to-man without getting all hot-under-the-collar."

"I'm not sittin', and I have nothing to say, except you owe me the use of that dog."

Becky slides down off the swing. "You can't have him!" she says, her little neck thrust out, face all screwed up. She's sassing this big old man in the cowboy boots, but I notice she's got one hand still holdin' fast to Ma's skirt.

"Hush, Becky," Ma tells her.

"Judd," I say, trying my best to reason with him. "Even if we were to let you, Shiloh wouldn't go."

"He'd go, all right," says Judd. "Where is he?" And he gives a whistle.

Under the steps, Shiloh don't move. I wonder if he's even breathing.

"See?" chirps Dara Lynn. "He won't even come out!" and she points to the steps. I could have drowned Dara Lynn.

Judd goes over to the side and gets down on all fours. I'm just close enough I can smell the beer on his breath. Don't think he's drunk, but he's been drinking.

"Here, you!" Judd yells, and whistles again. "Come on outta there, boy! Come on!"

I'm wondering what Shiloh's thinking right now. Does he think I'm lettin' this man come get him?

Stay there, Shiloh, I whisper. But I'm remembering the way he looked first day I found him back in the weeds over near Judd's, crawling along on his belly. Only thing that brought him to me was to whistle. What if he's so scared of Judd, of what will happen if he doesn't obey, that he comes out? Am I going to just sit here and let Judd take my dog, even for ten days? Will Dad let him?

I'm glad to see that nothing's happening. Shiloh's probably scrunched up in the far corner beneath the steps as far away as he can get.

Judd gets up off his hands and knees, cussing to himself, and goes to get the clothes pole. He comes back with it, ready to poke my dog out.

"No!" I say again, and this time I stand up. "You ain't goin' after my dog with that pole."

"Now, Judd, put that down." Dad gets up too, and his voice is strong. "That dog belongs to Marty now and you don't have permission to take him. I know you're upset about your dogs getting loose, but acting this way is not going to help."

And Ma says, "We got a daughter with a bite on her arm, but we're not going to press charges, so there's no 'cause for us to be mad at each other."

Judd stands there a full fifteen seconds, the pole in his hand. He glares at Dad. Then at me. He even glares at Ma and the girls.

Suddenly he throws the clothes pole to the ground.

"I ain't through with you, Ray Preston," he says. "I know you and that boy are behind this, I'll bet a week's pay. You ain't heard the last from me, you ain't seen the last, and I'm tellin' you now you'll be sorry."

He goes back across the yard, gets in his pickup, turns

around on our grass, and with a loud roar and a squeal of tires, he barrels on down our driveway, the dust from the gravel rolling off to the left.

Shiloh creeps out and comes up the steps, tail between his legs. He huddles against me, 'bout as close as he can get, and I put my arm around him.

We don't say a word, none of us. Just sit there watching that cloud of dust till Judd gets out to the road again and makes his turn.

Twelve

Everybody's talking about Judd's dogs the next day on the school bus. Dara Lynn, of course, had to go up and down the aisle showing off the place where Judd's black-and-white dog had bit her. To hear Dara Lynn tell the story, it had her arm in its teeth and had twisted it almost off before Ma whacked the dog with the clothes prop.

It was Michael Sholt's daddy who caught the black-and-white dog. After that the two other dogs scattered and were soon picked up. Michael's daddy said if someone else hadn't let loose Judd's dogs, he might have been mad enough to do it himself, on account of Judd's running into his mailbox twice. Guess there were a lot of folks starting to get mad at Judd Travers.

We all felt bad about the cat, though. Belonged to Mrs. Donaldson over there near Judd. Sarah heard that the cat had just been sitting out on the steps, sunning itself, when those dogs got hold of it and broke its neck. I reckon Mrs. Donaldson buried it back in her private cemetery with the rest of the Donaldsons. Don't know how many of 'em were cats.

Fred Niles heard that it was the man who'd got in a fistfight with Judd down in Bens Run who went up there and turned those dogs loose while Judd was at work, but I don't know that anyone could prove it.

David Howard's imagination gets going, though, it just never stops. After he got on the bus and heard the story about Mrs. Donaldson's cat and Dara Lynn's arm and the man from Bens Run, he says, "If those dogs snatched up a cat, they could snatch up a baby."

"What baby?" I say.

David shrugs. "Any baby! I'm just saying they *could*. What if someone put a baby out in a carriage and when they came back it was gone? If we hear of any baby missing, I'll bet Judd's dogs took it."

By the time that bus rolls into the driveway at school, we have cats missing, babies missing, girls with their arms torn clear off their bodies, and a whole pack of men from Bens Run all out lookin' for Judd Travers.

I'm still thinking about Judd's dogs, though. Wonder if once they start running in a pack like that and get a taste of blood, you can really change 'em. I'd like to put that in my report if I could, so when I get home from school I call John Collins.

I have to wait for him to come to the phone, his assistant tells me, 'cause he's working on a dog with a snake bite. But when he answers, I ask him about pack dogs, and can even a dog as mean as that be changed? How would a vet go about doing that?

"It's harder," says the vet, "but I've seen it done. What

you have to do, once you separate the dogs, is work with them one at a time. Sometimes when a dog is really mean and hiding out somewhere, you start by leaving food where he can reach it. He may not take it right away, but by and by he'll get hungry. Once he starts accepting your food, he'll listen for the sound of your voice and get to know you. And after he learns to trust you, he'll let you pet him. Just takes time. You have to be patient."

I thank John Collins and put it all in my report.

Since the whole class is still talking about Judd at school the next day, Miss Talbot asks us the difference between truth and gossip.

Truth, she says, is what you see with your own eyes and hear with your own ears. Gossip you get secondhand. Gossip may or may not be true, because it's coming to you from another person. It could even be *half* true, with parts left out now and then, and little extras tacked on to give it flavor.

I think about that a while, and then I figure there's another difference: truth's more important, but gossip's more interesting.

David Howard and me both get good grades on our reports because we actually talked to a forest ranger and a veterinarian.

When the bell rings for recess, though, Miss Talbot says, "Marty, I wonder if I could see you for a few minutes?"

What can you say but yes, so after everyone else goes out to play kickball, I got to sit over at the reference table where Miss Talbot's waiting for me.

After I sit down I see that she has my report in front of her, and there are big red circles all over it. She don't look mad, though.

"Marty," she says, "you and I come from the same kind of families, where the talk is slow and quiet and as soft and beautiful as a summer day. But it's not the way most people talk. If you spell the way you speak, people might have trouble reading what you write."

Then she shows me all the words she's circled in red—all the places where "don't" should be "doesn't," and "nothin'" should be "nothing" and "ain't" should be "aren't" or "isn't" and I don't know what all.

"It's okay to talk like that at home," she says. "That's personal talk; family talk. When I go back to my grandma's down in Mississippi, and we're all sitting around relaxed and happy, my tongue just slips into that easy way of talking, and everyone there knows exactly what I mean."

She smiles at me and I smile back.

"The problem," Miss Talbot says, "is that when you talk one way at home and another way at school, you've just got to be more careful, that's all. If you want to go to college and become a veterinarian, then you have to learn to speak and write and spell correctly."

Any other time a teacher told me to stay behind at recess, I would be thinking I was in big trouble. But when I leave the room and go out to get in that kickball game, I feel like Miss Talbot really wants to see me make something of myself.

"What'd you do, Marty, break a window?" Fred Niles calls out.

"Naw. She just wanted to talk about my report," I say.

The problem at our house now is that Dad's so quiet. I hardly ever seen him this quiet for so long. Looks to me like he can't put his mind to anything because he's troubled by something else. He sits down to watch TV and after a while you see his eyes are looking out the window, not at the screen.

"Sure wish this mess with Judd was cleared up," he says that Sunday out on the porch. It's getting cold now. You sit out too long, you'll need a coat. Couple weeks more and we won't be sitting out on the swing at all. "You were right, Marty," Dad goes on. "Maybe if we'd invited Judd to dinner before this thing got out of hand, we could have talked it out and come to some agreement. Yesterday he saw me pause at his mailbox, and he called, 'You just put that mail in there, Ray, and move along. Got no interest in talking to you.'"

"Somebody put his mailbox back up?"

"I expect Judd did. Nobody else was going to do it."

Knowing my dad, I figure he'll think of some way to patch things up with Judd Travers. Never saw a problem yet he couldn't lick. Only thing is, his job is a whole lot tougher now that Judd's mad. And *my* worry is that whatever they decide, if they *do* agree to something, they might make Shiloh part of the deal.

Seeing Dad worry reminds me of the way I felt when I was working for Judd, worrying that even after I'd put in my twenty hours, he still might not let me have the dog.

It was blackmail, pure and simple—me telling Judd that if I didn't get Shiloh I'd report the doe. I'd never in this world have done that if it weren't for Shiloh, and me wanting to save him.

It's the same with Dad. He'd let a neighbor hunt on his land before he'd work up a quarrel. But when it comes to protecting his children, Dad did and said things that weren't like him at all. Now all of us just seem to be sitting around waiting for what'll happen next.

"Dad," I say. "No matter what happens, you won't make me give back Shiloh, will you?"

Dad grunts and shakes his head, but I sure would have felt better if he'd come right out and said no.

Couple nights later at the supper table, Becky looks around and asks, "Why are we so quiet?"

"*I'm* not quiet!" says Dara Lynn, ready for some action. "You can talk to me, Becky."

"Want to hear my ABC song?" Becky asks.

"Becky, don't talk with your mouth full," says Ma. "Here. I want you to eat a little spinach with your meat."

Becky stares down at her spinach. "It looks like poop," she says.

"Becky!" scolds Ma.

Dara Lynn giggles so Becky says it again.

I guess Ma figures she's got to rescue the dinner conversation before it gets any worse, so she says to Dad, "I heard from Hettie today."

"What now?" says Dad, trying to liven up a little, too. Smiles. "They put Grandma in solitary confinement or something?"

"She *escaped?*" asks Dara Lynn.

"Dara Lynn, your grandma's not in prison," Ma says.

"Well, what'd she do?" I ask.

"Stealing again," says Ma.

"Money?" I ask.

Ma looks at Dad. "Teeth. False teeth."

Suddenly we just can't help ourselves. We all burst out laughing. The thought of Grandma Preston rolling her wheelchair from room to room and swiping people's false teeth is just too much to hold in.

"How'd they know she was *doing* it?" asks Dad.

"The nurse tried to talk to her but Grandma Preston wouldn't open her mouth. They finally got an orderly to help pry her lips open, and she had two pairs of teeth in there, her own and her neighbor's."

Dad is laughing so hard he's got tears in his eyes. I think part of me is feeling bad because we know Grandma Preston didn't mean to be this way at all and it sounds like we're making fun of her. But the other part of me says that sometimes things can happen that are sad and funny both. You can feel sad that her mind is gone, and still laugh at the stuff that's funny.

The laughter helps. I notice that when Dad's drying the dishes for Ma later, she's singing, and I know by the way Dad watches her that he likes to hear her sing.

And I'm feeling right angry at Judd Travers just then. Thinking how if it wasn't for him, we'd be like this every night: Happy.

It still ain't—isn't—too cold to romp around outside with Shiloh, so I take him for a run. Every so often I just got to test his legs. I go down the front steps and stand there beside my dog.

"Ready . . . !" I sing out, and Shiloh looks up at me. "Get set . . ." Shiloh's body starts to quiver. "Go!" I yell, top of my lungs.

We go racing down our driveway like a pack of wolves is on our heels. Guess maybe I'm testing my legs as much as Shiloh's, 'cause all the while I'm running, I'm counting by fives real slow, trying to get down as far as Doc Murphy's by the time I reach two hundred. Never done it yet. Two hundred thirty-five is closest I've come, but I figure if I keep practicing, I'll do it one of these days. Hate to say so, but I'll bet Dara Lynn could do it now. She can outrun me, but it's probably 'cause her legs are so skinny.

Road's near empty this hour of evening—everybody home eating supper—so it's a good time to practice our run. Shiloh's ahead of me, and he seems to know right where we're headed. I got sweat dripping from my eyeballs, almost, but Shiloh's going like a wind-up toy. Just won't stop. By the time we get to Doc Murphy's place, though, his sides are heaving.

We sit down on a log to rest. It's an old telephone pole, I think, that Doc rolled out there near the road to keep cars from cutting across the corner of his lot. I'm sitting there sweating something fierce, and Shiloh's on the ground, 'bout six feet away, his tongue hanging out, little drops of saliva dripping off the end. I got to be sure he's got plenty of water in his bowl when we get back, I'm thinking.

Shiloh looks at me like, "Is it time to go home yet?" and I say, "In a minute, Shiloh." Want to get rid of the ache in my side first. I wipe one arm across my forehead, and I'm just about to get up, when . . .

Pow!

Something hits the log so hard it jolts, and I don't know whether it's the log moving under me or the noise, but I tumble backward onto the ground. Shiloh hops over the log and scrunches down beside me. I know even before I can think it that somebody took a shot at us.

My heart's already pounding hard from the run, and now it's like to explode. Don't know whether to stay where we are or try to crawl up to Doc's house. Didn't see any lights on at his place, so he's probably not even home. I'm afraid if I try to move, Shiloh will make himself a target for whoever's out there.

And then I hear the sound of an engine starting up. I know, as I lie there, leaves in my face, that it's Judd Travers's pickup turning around on the road and heading back over the bridge.

It's only when the truck is gone that I sit up. I crawl back over the log again, looking for the place the bullet hit, and I find it—a small hole as round and clean as a gun barrel.

I let out my breath and pull Shiloh onto my lap. I can feel my knees shaking. Judd must have been coming over the bridge when he saw me and Shiloh racing down the road. He probably pulled over, got out, and followed us with his rifle.

There are three main thoughts going through my head, all trying to get my attention at the same time: first, this is the closest Judd ever came to trying to hurt Shiloh or me; second, I don't know whether he was trying to kill one of us, but his aim was way off the mark, so maybe he was only trying to scare me—either that or he's drunk; and third, I'm not tellin' my dad.

I can't. Tonight for the first time in a long while I heard my dad laugh, and telling him this wouldn't help nothing. Dad's going to patch things up with Judd; I know he will. In the meantime, though, I'm going to stick near our house. Keep myself and Shiloh off the main road altogether, especially at night. Don't want to give Judd any excuse whatsoever to try again.

Thirteen

I got to go to Doc Murphy's on Saturday, though, to help him lay some slab side timbers along his garden out back. There's something in me seems to be growing bigger and bigger and I feel I just can't hold it in no longer. It's not Judd taking a shot at me, neither.

So when Doc and I take a break—he's got this jug of fresh cider on his back steps—I take a sip from my glass and say, "I done something I shouldn't have done, but if I had it to do over, I don't know that I'd do any different."

Doc glances over at me, then takes a good long drink. "Well, we've all got a story or two like that, I guess."

"Not like mine," I say, and the more I talk the more I'm feeling this *has* to come out. If I don't tell it, it'll rip a hole in my chest.

I swallow. Swallow again. "You know how . . . after the German shepherd tore into Shiloh and we're taking care of him till he gets better? Well, I went up to Judd Travers the

Sunday I was supposed to give Shiloh back. I went up early morning to tell him I wanted to keep that dog. I was ready to do whatever it took to get Shiloh for my own. Even fight Judd, if I had to. I wasn't going to give him back."

Doc's giving me a puzzled look, like how can an eleven-year-old boy fight a two-hundred-pound car mechanic? Something I hadn't figured out either, to tell the truth.

"What happened, though, I came across Judd out in a field and I saw him kill a deer. A doe."

"In summer? He killed a doe?"

"Just shot it with his rifle. It wasn't anywhere near his garden, the way he said."

"There's a real stiff fine for that," Doc says.

"I know. I blackmailed him."

Doc sets down his glass of cider, arms resting on his knees and he looks at me for a long time.

"Judd's not real happy when I step out of the woods and he knows I seen him do it. I tell him that doe's not in season, and he wants to know what I'm going to do about it. I say I can tell the game warden, and he offers to divide the meat with my family if I keep quiet about it."

"Hmm," says Doc.

"I tell him I don't want that meat, I want Shiloh. So, the deal is I'll help him drag that doe to his place, keep my mouth shut, and work for him for two weeks. After that the dog's mine. So I do. And I never told my dad."

"I see," says Doc.

"Now you tell me something," I say. "Which do you suppose is right? Tell the game warden about that deer, and have to turn Shiloh back over to Judd? I never saw a dog so scared of a man as Shiloh was of him."

"Well, it seems to me, Marty, that you thought it over and did what you thought was best."

"But was it *right?*" I ask. "I didn't report Judd killing a deer out of season, and now I suppose he'll go right on doing it. Dad says he's been hunting some up in our woods lately, even though we got it posted. Might even be going up there drunk. What if he gets to firing crazy and one of his bullets comes down and kills Becky?" I take a deep breath. "Sometimes I don't sleep so good, just worrying about it."

What I don't tell Doc is that maybe if I'd reported Judd, they would have taken his rifle away, and then what Judd did out on the road last night wouldn't have happened. I don't guess they'd take his gun, though.

"Some folks," Doc's saying, "think they know what's right for every occasion. They say there's a right and wrong for everything. Well, it's good if things work out that way, but sometimes they don't."

"Even for you?" I ask.

Doc smiles just a little. "Especially for me. I grew up learning to tell the truth, Marty. My dad ever caught me in a lie, I'd get a whipping. Went through high school and college and medical school, and never once cheated on a test. The real tests, it seems, came later."

I realize I'm getting paid for sitting here in the shade on Doc's steps, drinking cold cider and listening to him talk, but he don't—doesn't—seem to care.

"There were a lot of them . . . tests. But not like the ones you get in school. There was a man with a sickness I couldn't cure. I knew that most people like him didn't have much time left to live. But he kept talking about how he was going to get well, and his wife said she knew he was going to get well, too, and when they asked me how he

90

was doing, I'd just . . . I'd just beat around the bush. Figured I wasn't going to be the one to make them sad."

"And then . . . ?"

"He died. Got real sick on a Sunday and was gone by Monday. Hadn't left a will. Hadn't taught his wife to drive or what to do about his business. And the wife came to me and said, 'Why didn't you *tell* us he was going to die? It would have made things so much easier.'"

"But you thought . . ."

"Yes, but I thought wrong. So when I had another patient I couldn't cure, I decided to tell her the truth. She was a painter. Had shows all over the state—Huntington, Charleston, Morgantown—even in New York City. I knew she didn't have a lot of time left, and figured she must have a lot of business to take care of. So the next time she was in my office talking about some pain she was having, I told her, as gently as I could, that she ought to get her affairs in order because she might not make that next big show she was talking about."

Here Doc takes a deep breath and puts his elbows on the step behind him.

"Well, she died five months later, and her friends sent me an angry letter. Why did I have to tell her? they asked. She was working on three paintings, her very best work, and after I told her the news, she never picked up her brush again. Just sat at home with the blinds drawn for five months and then died."

I sat thinking about that. "Maybe you could have said something sort of in-between," I suggested.

"Oh, I've tried that, don't think I haven't. I say, 'Only God knows when we're going to die.' Said that to a man just the other day and he looks me right in the eye and says, 'I know, Doc, but in your experience, how long does a man as

91

sick as me usually live?' Could hardly ask it plainer than that. Yet I wonder, does he really want to know?"

Doc picks up his glass again and drains it. "If folks know what's right and wrong for themselves, I've no quarrel with that. And we've all got to obey the law. But beyond that, what's right in one situation may be wrong in another. *You* have to decide. That's the hard part."

I realize when I go home that afternoon that Doc never did tell me what I should have done about that doe. And I see that no matter how old you get, you'll always meet up with problems and they won't have easy answers.

David Howard calls.

"Why don't you come over tomorrow?" he says. "I got this puzzle last year for my birthday that I never opened—a map of the ocean floor."

That's the kind of presents David's folks give him. No wonder he never opened it.

"You know how deep the deepest place in the ocean is?" asks David.

"No."

"Guess."

"A mile?"

"Almost *seven* miles!"

"You're lying, David."

"Come over tomorrow and see. Come around two o'clock and I'll show you. There're mountains and valleys on the floor of the ocean just like there are on land."

It was sounding more interesting now. "Okay," I tell him. "I'll come."

Dara Lynn's feeling good 'cause she's only got four more days to wait to see if Judd's black-and-white dog has rabies, and it don't look like he does. So she probably won't have to have shots. She's sliding around the kitchen in her stocking feet, pretending she's on ice skates, and then she grabs Becky's hands, and they're both slipping and sliding on Ma's waxed floor.

"Fine with me," says Ma, eating an apple in our living room. "They'll just shine it up all the prettier."

They have to get Shiloh into the act, though, and pretty soon they're trying to put Becky's socks on his paws and then they got a pair of Dara Lynn's underpants on him and a "Wild and Wonderful West Virginia" T-shirt. They're screeching and giggling and looking around for a cap and some sunglasses. I figure any dog who puts up with all that should get a medal of honor.

Dad comes home with news. Heard on his mail route today that Judd Travers went to work drunk one day this week, and his boss tells him it better not happen again.

Seems like every new thing Judd does is worse than the one before. First he runs into mailboxes. Then he picks a fight. Drives drunk and goes to work drunk. Maybe he'll get fired and move away from here, I'm thinking, and that would be just fine with me. Meanwhile, I'm not going out there on the road any more than I have to, and I'm not telling Dad what happened, neither. Dad would go see Judd and end up making him madder, and maybe he'd shoot at Becky next.

I sit up late that night watching TV with Ma and Dad. The nice thing about having the couch for my bed is I get to stay up as late as they do. That's not very late, of course, 'cause Dad starts his mail route early, so he's always in bed by ten o'clock. Saturdays, though, he'll stay up till eleven.

'Course, you don't get many TV channels up here above Friendly, unless you have a satellite dish, which we don't. So on Saturday nights we either all watch TV together, or Ma and Dad sit out in the kitchen talking after I spread out my blankets on the couch.

Lately Dad's been talking some of selling off a few acres of our land and maybe building on another room to our house—a new bedroom for him and Ma. Then I could have their old one. I'd like that. Seems like everyone who wants to live up here already does, though, so nobody's much interested in our land.

I'm lying on the couch thinking how it would be to have a room, just Shiloh and me in it together. I'm wondering what rabbits Shiloh's sniffing out tonight. Or maybe he's with that black Labrador and they're exploring all over the place. I listen to the sounds of our house after Ma and Dad go to bed—the refrigerator and the hot water heater, buzzing and clicking. I fall asleep about eleven thirty, I guess, dreaming of that puzzle of the ocean floor, and wondering if it's got mountains and valleys down there, like David says.

Then I hear the noise.

It's the kind of loud, scary noise that if you are sound asleep when you hear it, you think your heart is going to stop. You can't tell if your eyes are staring into the blackness of the room or the blackness inside your eyelids.

All you know is you hear something—a loud bang and then a thump and another and another.

You are so scared your chest hurts. Your heart is beating so loud you can hear it. You can hardly breathe. Is somebody breaking in? Are you the only one awake? Why isn't your dad getting up? you wonder.

And then, an even worse sound than that.

Shiloh.

Fourteen

I don't think I can stand this again—Shiloh getting tore up by that German shepherd in the middle of the night. He ain't penned up now! Shiloh can run!

But there's the sound again, a dog sound, a yipping, yelping, dog noise, and it just won't stop.

Shiloh season?

I leap off the couch.

Dad and Ma are awake now, too, coming down the hall. I race over and turn on the porch light, expecting to see my dog with his ear half off, but Shiloh's not there. He's close by, though. I can tell.

"What is it?" asks Ma, pulling her arm through the sleeve of her robe.

"I don't know," I say, slamming my feet into my shoes. "I got to find him."

"Wait a minute," says Dad. "I'll go with you."

Ma gets the flashlight, hands it to me. Her hair is

all loose around her face, eyes sort of sleepy-surprised.

The Shiloh noise comes again and I just go cold all over. Could he be poisoned? But I wonder. It's not a whine, not a howl, not a bark—or maybe it's all three. More like talking, is what it is.

Dad comes out of the bedroom. He's pulled his pants on over his pajamas, and we both put on our jackets.

"Please be careful," says Ma.

We start down the driveway, but in two seconds I've started to run, and Dad trots along beside me.

"Did you hear that noise? That bang?" I ask.

Dad nods. "Couldn't figure out what it was. Thought maybe it was thunder, the way it rolled on. That dog's not afraid of storms, is he?"

"I never saw Shiloh afraid of a storm. Maybe there're hunters out," I say.

The sky's cloudy. When the moon breaks through, though, we can see pretty good. Nothing looks different or strange all along our driveway, but then we pick up Shiloh in the beam of the flashlight.

He's standing out on the road, and he's got his tail tucked between his legs like he's done somethin' really bad.

I run over and bend down.

"Shiloh!" I cry. "You hurt?"

That noise comes out of his throat again. Second time that night my heart almost stops beating. I run my hands over his head and ears. All over his body, feeling for wounds. Feel his legs and paws. No bones out of place.

He's not foaming at the mouth or anything. He keeps looking to the right, though, so Dad shines the light up the road.

I can see there's something in it—some small thing, a

'possum, maybe. We go over to check. Shiloh goes along with us a little way, but then he hangs back.

We get up to that big pothole in the road, just before the bridge, and I see that the thing I caught in the flashlight beam is an old muffler dropped off somebody's car, that's all.

"Don't see anything else," says Dad.

Shiloh's stopped still now, won't come any farther.

I shine my flashlight slowly all around the road, the bridge, and then we see the weeds over on the side. They're all mashed down like some big steamroller come by. There's something else in the weeds. We walk over. It's the rest of the muffler. I shine my flashlight on down the bank. There at the bottom is Judd's pickup, turned on its side.

"Oh, no!" breathes Dad.

We are scrambling down that bank. We can tell from the smell of oil and gasoline that the accident just happened. Engine's still hot. Then we know that was the bang we heard, Judd's pickup hitting the pothole and rolling over and over before it hit bottom.

I got to tell the truth, and the truth is that all the while I'm climbing down that hill behind Dad, same bank I scrabbled down with David Howard, lookin' for a cave, I'm thinking how if Judd could just be dead, our problems would be over. Wouldn't have to worry about his hunting on our land, wouldn't have to wonder if he'd drive by drunk some night and run over Shiloh. Wouldn't have to be scared he'd take another shot at me.

But as soon as the thought come into my mind, I'm ashamed, and saying, "No, Jesus, I didn't mean it."

If Jesus is getting one prayer from your lips and another

from your heart, which one is he going to pay attention to? That's the question.

We get to the bottom and Dad grabs the flashlight out of my hand and shines it on the truck. A man's leg is sticking out from underneath the cab of the pickup. The leg don't move.

I'm down on my hands and knees, trying to see into the cab. Dad gets down beside me and shines the light through the windshield.

Looks to me like Judd's upside down, pinned between the steering wheel and the side. Smells like a brewery in there.

Dad gets the door on top open and leans way in, feeling for Judd's wrist.

"I got a pulse!" he says.

Then he's making his way around to the other side, and pushes on the truck to see if he can rock it. "See that big old limb over there?" he says. "Drag it here, Marty, and wedge it under, right next to Judd's leg. He's going to lose that leg if we don't prop the truck up a little."

He rocks the truck again, and I get the thick part of the limb wedged under. Figure the door on Judd's side must have come open as the truck rolled.

"You run home and call emergency," he tells me. "Do it quick, Marty. And then you call Doc Murphy in case the rescue squad takes too long getting here. Tell Doc that Judd's still alive, but he's unconscious."

I run like the wind, Shiloh beside me. He's been waiting up on the road, won't come down. But now he thinks it's a game almost. Looks happy again.

All the while I'm running, though, I'm wondering: Did Judd see Shiloh trotting along the road and try to run him over? Put on the gas, maybe, and that's when he hit the pothole?

That's my guess. All I really know is that if Shiloh hadn't carried on like he did, I wouldn't never have got up. Would've laid there a while, maybe, wondering if that bang I heard was thunder, but I would have gone right back to sleep. If Judd lives, it's because of Shiloh.

Ma is standing at the screen, and Dara Lynn's beside her, rubbing her eyes and looking cross.

"Marty?" calls Ma.

"It's Judd!" I yell, more out of breath than I realize. "His truck went down the bank by the bridge. Call emergency, and then call Doc Murphy."

Ma finds another flashlight for me, and I go out to the road, wait until I see Doc's car coming real slow, looking for where it is he should stop.

Doc gets out at the bridge. He's got his pajamas on, too, and a robe on top. Got his black bag with him. I help him down the bank and through the weeds and brush to Judd's pickup. Dad's got the door open, and Doc leans way in with his stethoscope as best he can. Takes the flashlight and checks out Judd's eyes.

"Internal injuries, that's my guess," Doc says. "No way I can examine him without crawling in there, and doing more harm than good. . . ."

It's about then we hear the far-off sound of a siren, and I climb back up the bank to wait for them, show them where we are. I see that Shiloh didn't come back with me; stayed home with Ma and Dara Lynn.

Then there's lights and yelling and a truck motor running. Men are coming down the bank with a stretcher, the radio's blaring. Floodlights are turned on me and Dad and Doc, all in our pajamas. Nobody cares.

The pickup is gently set upright again. Splints are being

99

put on Judd's neck and back before they place him on the stretcher. Then the men are carrying him up the bank, and at some point Judd opens his mouth and groans. Says something, but all I can make out is a cuss word.

"Sure sounds like Judd Travers," one of the men says, and three minutes later the rescue truck is heading for the hospital in Sistersville.

Fifteen

I s he dead?"

First words out of Dara Lynn's mouth when we get back to the house.

"No, but he's unconscious," Dad says, and tells them what happened.

"What about his truck?" Ma asks.

"Whelan's will send up a tow truck tomorrow."

"Do you think he's badly hurt, Ray?"

"Likely so. Got a broken leg, I can tell you that."

"Was the bone all sticking out?" asks Dara Lynn. I tell you, I got the strangest sister.

"All I know is that the truck came down on it when it turned over," Dad says.

Dara Lynn sticks around long enough to see if there're any more gory details, then ambles off to bed. Becky, of course, sleeps through the whole thing.

Ma and Dad talk a little more out in the kitchen, then

turn off the light and go back to bed. I lay on the couch, staring up into the dark. I'm having this conversation with Jesus again, only I'm doing all the talking. One minute I hope He's listening, and the next minute I hope He's not.

"Help him get well," I'm saying, because I think I should. Because you're supposed to pray for somebody who's been hurt.

Then I find myself thinking, *Just don't let his leg get well enough to ever go hunting again*.

Can you ask God to heal things, but only so much?

Next morning a tow truck comes up from Whelan's, and people stand around to watch. It's Sunday morning, so word hasn't spread too far yet. Dad and me and Dara Lynn all go over to watch—Dad wants to be sure there's nothing left in the weeds belonging to Judd. Finally the truck's up on the road again, being towed to the garage where Judd works. Truck don't look as bad as Judd did. Bet he didn't even have his seat belt on.

After Sunday dinner, Dad drives me down to David Howard's, and soon as I see him out on the porch, I run up.

"You hear what happened?" I say. Can tell by David's face he hasn't.

"What?" he says.

"You know that big pothole this side of the bridge?"

"It caved in?" whoops David.

"No, but you know Judd's truck?"

"It fell through?"

"No, David, let me tell it! Judd was driving drunk again last night, and his truck must of hit the pothole and gone out of control."

Then I tell him how the sheriff figures it hit the bridge first, then rolled on down the bank, Judd with it.

"Wooooow!" says David Howard, and the way he says it, dragging it out, sounds like air coming slow out of a bag.

We go in and tell his folks, and Mr. Howard calls his newspaper to be sure they've got the story.

David and I work at putting together his puzzle of the floor of the Pacific Ocean. Takes about two hours, with Mrs. Howard helping sometimes, and when we're all done, all we've got is a lot of light and dark lines; looks like blue burlap up close, with names printed on it: Galapagos Fracture Zone, Continental Shelf, Bounty Trough, Bonin Trench. Heck, I figured there would be fish and pirates' treasure chests and sunken ships on the bottom, not just lines.

Mrs. Howard, though, she's pointing out the Marianas Trench on the map.

"That's the world's greatest ocean depth," she says. "Almost seven miles deep."

I'm thinking what it would be like to go seven miles straight down in the ocean. Ma's granddaddy worked in a coal mine, but he didn't go down any seven miles. Quarter mile, maybe, and that's scary enough.

Dad was supposed to pick me up at four but it's almost four thirty when he shows up. I don't mind, 'cause Mrs. Howard gets out some pumpkin pie, and this gives me time for a second piece.

When I get in the Jeep, Dad says, "Didn't mean to be late, but I drove down to the hospital to look in on Judd. Took longer than I thought. Doctor wanted to talk to me."

"What'd he say?"

"Wanted to know if Judd had any relatives around here, and I couldn't think of a one."

"How is he?"

"They operated on him last night. Had some internal injuries, like Doc Murphy said. Ruptured spleen, couple broken ribs, left leg broken in two places, fractured collarbone, skull fracture. . . . Still, his condition is stable."

"He's going to live, then?" I sure didn't sound very pleased.

"I think so. But it's going to be a while before he can go back to work."

"How about hunting?" I ask.

"That I don't know, son."

Then I know I have to do it.

"Dad," I say. "I got something to tell you." I swallow.

Dad looks over at me, and then he pulls the Jeep off the road and turns off the engine. Don't say nothing. Just sits there studying me.

I take a big breath and tell him everything. Tell him how I'd blackmailed Judd into giving me Shiloh by promising not to report him to the game warden. And when I get all that out of my system, I tell him about Shiloh and me out on the road by Doc Murphy's, and how I'm pretty sure it was Judd who took a shot at us.

Didn't exactly plan it this way, but when you got two things to tell, one of 'em scarier than the other, it's the scary one your dad will fix on every time.

"He *shot* at you, Marty?" he says. "He *shot* at you and you never told me?" He's so worked up he forgets all about the blackmail. "Why *didn't* you tell me?"

" 'Cause I didn't see it would help. Just make you mad and Judd madder. I figured I'd stay clear off the road till we got this thing settled."

Dad tips back his head and closes his eyes.

"Marty," he says finally. "Sometimes I'm stubborn and sometimes I'm cross, but don't you ever keep something like this from me again. Somebody takes a shot at one of my children, I want to hear about it. I want you to *promise* . . ."

"I promise," I say, quicker than he can blink.

And when Dad starts up the engine again and don't say one word about the blackmail, I'm so happy and relieved to have it out and over with I almost start to whistle. Then I figure that with a man in the hospital, half his bones broke, it's no time to be whistling, no matter *what* I think of him.

It's the talk of the school on Monday. Everybody's heard by then, and everyone's added a little something extra to the story.

"You hear about Judd?" says Michael Sholt. "Drove his truck right off the bridge and into the creek."

"Split his head wide open," says Fred Niles.

Sarah Peters says Judd's dogs were with him and all of 'em drowned, and by the time the bus pulls into the school yard, we got Judd Travers dead and buried already, dogs along with him. I see now the difference between truth and gossip.

Miss Talbot tries to sort out fact from fancy, but because I'm the only one who really saw Judd lying inside his truck, she takes my version and says we'll find out later what the newspaper has to say.

Then she says it might be nice to make a big card and send it to Judd from our sixth-grade class. The thing about folks from the outside is that as soon as they move to where we live, they want to change things—make them better. And there's nothing wrong with that, I guess, except she don't—doesn't—understand how long we've been hating Judd Travers.

The room is so quiet you can hear Michael Sholt's

stomach growl. Fact is, it might be "nice" to make a card, but there's not a single person wants to sign it.

Miss Talbot senses right away what the problem is. She says that the wonderful thing about the English language is there are enough words to say almost anything at all, and if you don't want to say something one way you can say it another.

"What could we say that would be both helpful and honest?" she asks.

"We hope you get well?" says Sarah, but the rest of us shake our heads. Nobody wants him driving drunk along the road anytime soon.

"We're sorry about your accident?" says David.

But the truth is we're not. Nothing else seemed able to stop Judd Travers from knocking over mailboxes and backing his truck into fences. He could have run over Shiloh.

Finally I raise my hand. "What about 'Get Well'?" I say.

We vote for that. It's more like a command than a wish. Miss Talbot gets out this big sheet of white drawing paper and folds it in half. On the outside, in big green letters, she writes, "Get Well!" And on the inside, in different colored pens, we take turns signing our names.

Some of the girls draw flowers at the ends of their names. Fred Niles draws an airplane, which don't make a bit of sense. When it comes my turn, I do something I didn't plan on, but somehow it seems right: I put down two names: *Marty and Shiloh.*

By the time Judd comes home from the hospital, the leaves are beginning to fall. Halloween's come and gone. (I was a pizza and David was a bottle of ketchup.) Judd's black-and-white dog didn't have rabies, and the county says they'll keep it until Judd can take care of his dogs himself.

The neighbors on one side of Judd took one of his other two dogs to care for, and the neighbors on the other took the third. Still another neighbor drives his tractor mower over to Judd's and mows his grass, and Whelan's Garage fixes his truck up for him and parks it in front of his house for when he's ready to drive again. All the dents are gone.

It was Dad who drove Judd home from the hospital. Ma had shopped the day before and sent along two big sacks of groceries. Dad helped Judd get into the house with them.

Told us later that Judd said hardly a single solitary word to him the whole time. Just sat looking straight ahead. Got his neck in a brace, of course, and a big old cast on his leg. Sits without turning left or right because his ribs are mending.

"Did you tell him we were the ones who found him?" I ask.

"I did," says Dad, "but it didn't seem to make much difference to him, one way or another."

I rake leaves at Doc Murphy's that Saturday. He asks if I know how Judd is doing.

"Ma says there's a visiting nurse comes twice a week," I tell him.

Doc shakes his head. "Some people seem to have a string of bad luck they can't do anything about, and other folks have a string of bad luck all their own doing," Doc says. "Guess Judd's had a little of both."

I can only think of the kind he got himself into. "What's the kind he couldn't do anything about?" I ask.

"Getting born into the family he did," says Doc.

"Did you know 'em?"

"Knew who they were. Lived in a house couple miles from here, other side of the creek. Mostly I heard stories from some of my patients, but the stories were so much alike there was bound to be a little truth in them."

"What did they say?"

"Mostly about old man Travers beating his kids. They get out of line, he'd take a belt to them. The buckle end, mind you. Neighbors said they could hear those kids yelling sometimes clear down the road. Once or twice somebody called the law, but nothing much was done."

"What happened to them? Where did they all go?"

"Most of the kids ran away as soon as they could, moved away, or got married. Judd was the youngest, and when the others left and old man Travers got peeved, Judd got his share of it and the others' share as well. Then there was a fire, and that house went up like a torch. Mrs. Travers died, but Judd got out, and his dad, too, but old man Travers died a week later of a heart attack. That's when Judd moved on down the road into that rental trailer. Been there ever since. Far as I know, he doesn't have a girlfriend. Hardly any men friends either. Just him and those dogs, and the way he treats 'em, you could hardly call them friends."

"You'd think that a man who missed out on kindness would want to be kind to his dogs," I say.

"You have to *learn* kindness, Marty, same as you learn to tie your shoes," Doc says. "And Judd just never had anyone to teach him."

I think about that a lot. All I can figure is that Judd would rather be the grown-up who does the beating, not the kid who's getting beat. Doesn't seem to realize they ain't—aren't—the only two choices he's got.

That afternoon when Dad comes home from delivering the mail, I ask if maybe we can go visit Judd.

"I don't think I'd try it, Marty," he says. "I've been taking his mail right up to his door so he don't have to climb down those steps to get it. I always rap on the door, ask how he's doing. I know he's there. But he never answers. Neighbors tell me he does the same with them."

"You figure he'll stop drinking now?"

"I doubt it, but I hope I'm wrong. They say a man has to reach bottom before he stops. If this isn't bottom, I'd sure hate to see what is."

What I'm wondering is whether Judd looks in the mirror each morning and decides he can't stand what he sees. Never wanted a dog that was lame in any way. Never wanted a dent or a scratch in his pickup. Now it's him that has the scratches and bruises and broken bones. I heard a couple men talking about how Judd might get it in his head just to shoot himself, and I'm wondering how I'd feel if he did.

Don't know that I'd be too sorry, 'cause once he's well, we got the very same problems we had before. Judd'll be just like he was, only meaner.

Sixteen

The next day, though, just because I ask, Dad and I get in the Jeep and drive over to Judd's. Seems strange to park across the road from his trailer and not be greeted by a bunch of yelping, snarling hounds.

November sun is shining down on Middle Island Creek, and you'd never think that inside that trailer is a man as wretched and mean and sad as a man can get. His grass has been mowed again, probably for the last time this year, but all his shades are pulled, like he don't want one ounce of sunlight trying to sneak its way into his house and cheer him up.

We start across the road to where Judd's board sidewalk begins. The trailer door opens. There is Judd, big cast on his leg, holding his shotgun.

"What you want, Ray Preston?" he calls. Still wearing a neck brace, I see.

We stop dead still. "Marty and I just wanted to stop by, say hello," Dad calls back.

"Well, I don't need no hellos," Judd says. He's not exactly pointing the gun at us, but he's not pointing it away, neither.

"You need any groceries, Judd? Anything I can pick up for you?" Dad asks.

"Don't need nothing."

"Well . . . okay. We're just concerned about you. Everyone is."

Judd gives this little laugh—so weak you could hardly call it that—and closes the door again.

"Well, son?" says Dad. "Looks like that's that."

But something in me just don't give up. If kindness has to be learned, then maybe Judd's got some lessons coming. If I don't try, and Judd ever hurts Shiloh, how am I going to feel then?

Soon as we get home, I say, "Ma, you suppose we could fix up something every day to leave there on the steps along with Judd's mail? Something to eat?"

"I think that's a fine idea, Marty," she says. "When I was making bread this morning, I was thinking of giving him some."

That evening, I wrap up a loaf for Judd, and next day Dad takes it along with him and puts it right outside Judd's door.

On Tuesday, though, Dad reports that the bread he'd left on Monday's still there. Judd had taken in his mail but left the bread outside. And you know what I'm thinking? It's not just the world he's mad at; he's mad at himself. Oh, it's partly that he don't want to take any kindness from the Prestons, 'cause he don't—doesn't—know how to give any back in return. But when a man's sunk about as low as he can get, I'll bet he feels he don't even have a right to that bread.

"What did you do with the chicken I wrapped up for him this time?" I ask Dad.

"Just set it right there beside the bread," Dad tells me.

Well, I thought, just like John Collins says, you leave it there long enough, he'll get hungry.

On Wednesday, Dad says that both the bread and the chicken are gone. Judd could've thrown 'em out, of course, but sometimes you got to take chances.

"What kind of mail does he get?" I ask my dad.

"Oh, magazines, mostly. *Guns and Ammo. Shooting Times*. Junk mail, bills."

"He ever get any letters?"

"None I can remember."

After the first week of leaving food outside Judd's door, I decide I'll start sending a little note under the rubber band on the food package:

> *Last month a bee was chasing Shiloh. You should have seen him. Was running and looking behind him both at the same time, and he run into a bush. Thought that bee would drive him right down to the creek. Think Shiloh put his nose too close to a nest somewhere. He'll be a little more careful after this.*
> *Marty*

We weren't the only ones taking food to Judd. Heard that some of the neighbors had been leaving casseroles and cakes outside his door from time to time. The food

112

seemed to disappear, so we figure either Judd was eating it or burying it, one or the other.

Still, we wonder, what's a man thinking and feeling when he don't never come to the door, don't never say thank you, sits in his house all day with the shades pulled? Sits there hating himself, I'll bet. Knows if he keeps up the way he was doing, he'll lose his job, and then he'll lose everything—trailer, dogs, guns. . . .

Doc Murphy told me that he'd heard Judd was healing nicely. His body, that is. It would take some time for that leg to heal, but the visiting nurse said he was moving around a whole lot better than he had been.

I'm thinking about Shiloh and when I first saw him— all slunk down in the brush, so trembly and scared of me he couldn't stop shaking. Wouldn't even let me pet him—just crawled away on his belly. No trust left in him at all.

Thinking, too, of the other three dogs of Judd's— the way he'd chained them up, so fearful something or somebody was going to come along and start a fight they couldn't win. All snarlin' and snapping, trying to keep themselves from being hurt.

And now that we got Judd all shut up in his trailer, I'm thinking how slowly, a little bit at a time, we got to teach him kindness. He was taking the food we left for him. That was a start.

Seemed like the only thing I could think of to write about in my notes to Judd was about Shiloh. Thinking back on things, it was the only thing we both cared about, though I guess we cared about Shiloh in different ways.

I told him how much Shiloh weighed now, when we took him to the vet. How we're not supposed to feed him table scraps, but buy him this balanced dog food, make his coat shiny. Told how we laughed ourselves sick once watching Shiloh take off after a mole burrowing along just beneath the ground. Fast as Shiloh could dig, that mole was tunneling away from him. Every last thing Shiloh ever did that would interest a live body in the least, I put down on paper. I figure if a man don't get any other letters, he's got to be interested in the only ones he gets.

The blinds come up in Judd's trailer. Nobody's seen him at a window yet, but he can't hardly keep from seeing out.

One day I decide that all these notes I've been writing about Shiloh are just so much noise—just writing around and around what it is I really want to say to Judd. And what it is I want to say is that here's this little dog he kicked and cussed and starved, so scared of Judd he won't never even cross the bridge leading to the road Judd's house is on. Yet one night he meets up with Judd's truck out on the road. I still don't know whether Judd had been drunk and had hit the pothole the wrong way, or whether he'd seen Shiloh trotting down the road and was trying to hit him.

But here's this man pinned under his truck at the bottom of a bank, dead of night, quarter mile from any house except ours, and Shiloh could have sneaked on home without a sound. Judd could have died in the wreck that night. Might have, too. Nobody would have discovered him till the next morning. Maybe not even then.

But instead, the dog starts crying and whining, scared as he is of gettin' within a hundred feet of Judd Travers, and wakes us up. I don't expect Judd to jump up and down, I say in my letter. Shiloh don't expect no reward. Judd don't have to go around praising my dog. I just think he ought to

114

know that it wasn't my dad and me who saved him that night, it was Shiloh.

I stick the note under the rubber band on the raisin rolls I package up for Dad to put on Judd's doorstep the next afternoon.

A day goes by. Two days. And then, on a Friday afternoon when Dad gets home from work, I say to him, "I want to go see Judd Travers."

"Now, Marty," says Dad. He's still sitting in the Jeep. "You know what happened last time. What makes you think he'll let you in?"

"Nothin'. Just want to try, is all," I say. "I don't want to go on fighting with Judd and worrying myself sick about Shiloh."

"Well, hop in. Might as well go now as later," he says.

"Wait just a minute, I'm takin' something," I say. And I go back to the porch where Shiloh is sitting, happy as a beetle on a rosebud, and gather him up in my arms.

"We're goin' visiting," I say.

Shiloh licks my face.

I get in the Jeep, but I don't put Shiloh on the seat by Dad and crawl in the back, way I usually do. I fasten my seat belt and hold my dog in my lap.

Dad's giving me his puzzled look. "You sure about this, son?"

"No. But it's only a visit," I say.

Shiloh wriggles right over to the window and sticks his head out as Dad starts the motor.

"Be right back," I yell to Ma. She and the girls have their coats on, picking up black walnuts over by the shed.

Shiloh hangs out the window, one paw on the sill, and

the happier he looks, the more I wonder: Am I doing the right thing?

Shiloh's happiness lasts just till we get to the end of the driveway, because as soon as Dad turns right, he backs away from the window and looks up at me.

I stroke his head.

"It's okay, Shiloh," I say. I hold onto him, because I'm afraid when we go to cross the bridge he might try to jump out the window or something, run back home. I roll up the window. It's cold, anyway.

Dad eases the Jeep around the pothole, and as we start over the bridge, the boards makin' loose rattly sounds beneath the truck, Shiloh sinks down in my lap, like all the wind is going out of him.

"It's okay," I say again.

He licks my hand.

Once across the bridge, though, when we turn right again, Shiloh starts to whine—a high, soft whine down in his throat. I stroke his back. I'm remembering how, when he come to me for the first time, Dad made me take him back to his rightful owner. Owner, anyway. And how he had hunkered down on my lap, just like he's doing now.

I want in the worst way to let him know that this time is different. That I wouldn't let Judd have him for all the money in the world. Wouldn't never even loan him out. Just payin' a visit, is all. But there's no way Shiloh can understand. All he's got in his memory is the time I took him back before, and how Judd had kicked him when I let him out of the Jeep—kicked him and shut him up in his shed and didn't feed him for a couple days.

I swallow. Just hearing my dog whimper and feeling his body shake, I think, how can this be the right thing to do?

We get to Judd's and park on the creek side. Shiloh is really whimpering now, scrunched up on my legs like he's trying to grow roots.

I hug him in my arms as we get out.

"I'm not puttin' you down," I say. "You're mine for as long as you live. I promise you that."

He licks my face again.

We cross the road and go up the board sidewalk to Judd's trailer. Go up the steps.

Dad knocks on the door, and Shiloh snuggles up against me, don't make a sound. Figure he's thinking if he don't make any noise, Judd may not notice.

Nobody comes. I know Judd's there, 'cause I can hear the TV going.

Dad knocks again.

The TV goes off. Nothing happens.

"Judd," Dad calls. "Got a visitor here to see you."

Still no answer. I'm thinking maybe this is a sign that I should turn around right this minute and go back. Think maybe Judd is going for that shotgun. Will tell himself that if it wasn't for the dog, he wouldn't have started drinking heavy, and if he hadn't started drinking heavy, he wouldn't have hit that pothole the way he did, and if he hadn't hit the pothole, he wouldn't be laid up with a broken leg right now.

Then the door opens, but only a crack.

"What you want?" Judd's voice.

Shiloh is shaking so hard I think he is gonna shake right out of my arms.

"Got someone here to see you," Dad says pleasant-like, and steps aside. I move over to where Judd can see me through the crack in the door.

There is not a sound from inside, but the door don't close. Shiloh's grown bigger and fatter and sleeker since he became my dog, but right now, burrowed down almost as far as he can get in my arms, he looks almost like a pup.

"We just came for a visit," I say, to make it plain right off that no way am I giving Judd this dog.

And finally, when the quiet gets almost embarrassing, Judd opens the door a little wider. "Well, come on in for a minute," he says. And it's Judd who's embarrassed. First time in my life I ever saw a look on his face that says he's ashamed of himself.

First time I been in Judd's trailer, too. And the thing I notice is it smells. Smells like the home of a man who don't empty his garbage or wash his socks when he should.

I see he's not wearin' the neck brace anymore, but he still walks stiff, and he's still got this big cast on his leg.

He leans over and picks up some magazines on the couch, throws 'em on the floor. "Sit down, if you want," he says, and lowers himself into the straight-back chair beside the couch, broke leg out in front of him.

I'm trying to hold Shiloh as tight as I can to give him the message that he won't get loose. That I don't *want* him loose. But he's still shaking. Wouldn't surprise me none if he peed on my leg.

"It's good to see you up and around," Dad says, sitting on the couch beside me. "Things are healing all right, are they?"

"Doing okay," says Judd, his voice low. He don't take his eyes off Shiloh, though.

I wonder what he thinks about this scared, trembling dog, hunkered down on my lap, silent now and limp as a leaf. Wonder if he's thinking about when this dog was his—

the way he treated him then, the way Shiloh kept running away.

"So he's the one that found me," Judd says.

"Yeah," I tell him. "Just kept on making those noises till we come out and found your truck."

All the while I'm talkin', I'm rubbing Shiloh's silky head, scratching gently behind his ears, running my hand along his back, then starting all over again. Judd's watchin'.

"I suppose he remembers me," says Judd.

I don't answer. The way Shiloh's shaking, there's no doubt.

Judd leans forward a little, and I think I see his hand move. Slowly he reaches out, and I can feel Shiloh flinch. I swallow as I see him shy away, drawing back from Judd's touch.

But Judd lets his fingers rest lightly on top of Shiloh's head, just the way mine did. And then, he begins to stroke my dog.

At first I think Shiloh's too numb to feel it, too scared to breathe. All he wants to do, I know, is get out of there, make sure he's not going to be left behind.

I figure that Judd's going to give him a couple more strokes and pull his hand away, but he don't. Just keeps stroking Shiloh's head, like he's found somethin' here he needs, and I can begin to feel Shiloh's body easing up some, feel his legs relax.

He sits real still, looks straight ahead. Judd's strokes get more even, not so jerky. The palm of his hand strokes lower now, down on Shiloh's nose, then slowly moves up over the forehead, before the fingers settle behind Shiloh's ears and do a little gentle scratching.

I glance over at Judd, a quick little look, and for just a

moment, his eyes seem wet. I look down at my dog again. Don't want to embarrass Judd.

Does Shiloh know I wouldn't never leave him? That this is only a visit, and that he's mine forever and ever? I think he does, because the next time Judd's fingers come forward to stroke his head, Shiloh—for the very first time—reaches up and licks Judd's hand.